'So, were you sent to secure the deal in the time-honoured way?'

She stared at him with her mouth open.

'Don't play the innocent with me,' he advised softly. 'It happens. So what exactly does The Perfect Day wedding consultancy supply? Your services in my bed as well?'

Chas drew a deep breath into her lungs and swung her free hand so that it connected with his cheek, hard.

He didn't even flinch, but jerked her into his arms. 'If that's how you like it—rough—two can play that game,' he said, barely audibly.

His arms felt like iron bars around her. The look in his eyes, of serious contempt, frightened the life out of her. But what was even more frightening was the realisation that, contemptuous or not, he intended to kiss her...

Lindsay Armstrong was born in South Africa, but now lives in Australia with her New Zealand-born husband and their five children. They have lived in nearly every state of Australia and have tried their hand at some unusual–for them–occupations, such as farming and horse-training–all grist to the mill for a writer! Lindsay started writing romances when their youngest child began school and she was left feeling at a loose end. She is still doing it and loving it.

Recent titles by the same author:

THE RICH MAN'S VIRGIN
THE MILLIONAIRE'S MARRIAGE CLAIM
A BRIDE FOR HIS CONVENIENCE
THE AUSTRALIAN'S CONVENIENT BRIDE
THE UNCONVENTIONAL BRIDE

AT THE
CATTLEMAN'S
COMMAND

BY
LINDSAY ARMSTRONG

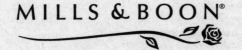

MILLS & BOON®

All the characters in this book have no existence outside the imagination of the author, and have no relation whatsoever to anyone bearing the same name or names. They are not even distantly inspired by any individual known or unknown to the author, and all the incidents are pure invention.

First published in Great Britain 2006
Harlequin Mills & Boon Limited,
Eton House, 18-24 Paradise Road, Richmond, Surrey TW9 1SR

© Lindsay Armstrong 2006

ISBN 0 263 84797 7

Set in Times Roman 10½ on 12pt.
01-0306-45705

Printed and bound in Spain
by Litografia Rosés, S.A., Barcelona

CHAPTER ONE

'CHAS BARTLETT?' Tom Hocking frowned. 'Are you suggesting a man to organise this wedding, Birdie?'

'Not so strange when you think about it,' his secretary, Birdie Tait, offered.

They were talking to each other over the phone, Tom from his stud outside Warwick, Birdie from the office in Toowoomba.

'Men do design clothes,' Birdie continued down the line. 'They also make great chefs and interior decorators, so—why not? Chas Bartlett certainly comes highly recommended.'

'You've met him?'

'No. But I spoke to a very satisfied customer. All Laura Richmond could say was Chas did this; Chas organised that; Chas was a dream! And her daughter's wedding was a howling success.'

'Laura Richmond,' Tom repeated thoughtfully. 'Talk about a raging snob if ever I've met one. Mind you, things are getting hairy up here, so…' He paused and shrugged. 'Go ahead and hire the guy, Birdie, for a consultation at least.' He pulled his diary towards him. 'Am I right in thinking I'm free next weekend?'

'Yes, Mr Hocking.'

'Then see if you can get him to drive up and stay overnight on Saturday; we'll all be here, which may not be that easy to arrange over the next few weeks. Explain that to him if he objects to working weekends.' He paused. 'It mightn't be a bad idea to drop the hint that my sister is marrying the heir to a peer of the realm.'

'A very good idea, Mr Hocking.'

'Thanks, Birdie. If I don't hear otherwise from you, I'll expect him at—say—four o'clock on Saturday afternoon?'

'I'll do my best, Mr Hocking.' Birdie put the phone down.

She was well-named but, although frail and diminutive in appearance, she had the heart of a lioness when it came to guarding and promoting her employer's interests. In many ways she looked upon Tom Hocking as the son she'd never had—she'd worked for his father Andrew and had been wildly and hopelessly in love with him.

Truth be told, she would have been much more interested in seeing Tom marry and settle down rather than his sister, Vanessa, whose wedding they'd been discussing—but here she often paused and sighed.

At thirty-three and six feet four in his socks with a rock-hard body, Tom attracted women in droves. It wasn't only that. He was equally at home riding a horse or flying a plane, and his business acumen had seen him advance the Hocking empire with a vengeance when he'd taken over from his father.

He now held executive positions on the boards of several companies that were Australian icons. He mixed—but then the Hockings always had—with the cream of society.

But was there more than the occasional tinge of impatience in his grey eyes, eyes that were often amused as well as devastatingly acute, these days? His sense of humour had always been wicked and irreverent, but when he lost his temper the wisest course was to take evasive action. Not that it happened often but—was it happening more often these days?

Birdie sighed again. She could tell that her boss wasn't a hundred per cent happy but there was nothing she could do to help.

She might like to pin it down to the lack of the right woman in his life but that was simplistic, she knew. On the other hand, finding the perfect woman could be part of the problem. Even at his best, Tom Hocking was a handful. He was a born leader and capable of sheer arrogance. One suspected a prospective wife would need the patience of a saint, but would a saint be what Tom was looking for?

Tom Hocking also took a moment to ponder after talking to Birdie on the phone.

It so happened he liked the heir to the peer of the realm to whom his sister, Vanessa, was engaged, but he wasn't totally convinced Rupert Leeton, Lord Weaver, was what she needed. Vanessa was as headstrong as an unbroken filly at times, whereas Rupert was a thinker and a dreamer.

His mother was ecstatic about it, though. Even his aunt Clare, a dedicated, rather eccentric spinster who lived with them, was delighted.

However, the run-up to these nuptials looked set to provide a maelstrom of confusion and turbulence.

Vanessa and his mother were already arguing over wedding-dress designers, venues and bridesmaids. Clare and Vanessa were at loggerheads over the choice of minister to perform the service. Rupert was starting to look strained and his slight stammer was becoming more pronounced.

Tom was of the opinion that it promised to be a rare

bun fight, unless he took a hand, hence his decision to call in a wedding consultant.

He pushed his fingers through his hair then rubbed his jaw as he contemplated his household and his life-style.

He'd stepped into his father's shoes five years ago. At that time Cresswell Lodge, on Queensland's Darling Downs, had been the main family enterprise. An historic thoroughbred stud pioneered by one of his ancestors, its beautiful old homestead was still a showpiece.

The stud sold yearlings all over the world and, in consequence, the Hocking family rubbed shoulders with the élite of the thoroughbred world: sheikhs, royalty and self-made billionaires from all continents.

Not only had he continued that tradition but he'd also branched out. He'd put his love of flying, brought with him from the air force, to good use, for example, and turned a small crop-spraying business into a private airline. Most of his customers were pastoralists, graziers or mining and exploration companies, but he'd recently opened a deluxe charter wing for anyone who wanted to get from A to B in style and privacy. It was going well. So were his other non-thoroughbred enterprises.

Not that his mother, Harriet, approved entirely. She gave the impression that anything tainted with commercial overtones, which encompassed just about everything that didn't have to do with horses, was beneath her. She lived and breathed horses. She had been a champion dressage rider in her day with an Olympic medal to her credit.

That was how Cresswell had acquired Rupert Leeton. The son of a friend of a friend of Tom's mother, he'd come 'down under' to further his Olympic equestrian aspirations by taking tutelage from Harriet Hocking—and he'd never left.

A frequent source of irritation for Tom was the way his mother, and his sister come to that, simply refused to recognise that Cresswell Stud was a highly commercial enterprise, even if it did rely on horses. It was his father's judgement in mares and stallions, and now his own, that kept an awful lot of dollars rolling in, without which they wouldn't be able to scour virtually the whole world for horses.

Vanessa was also horse-mad. She was a showjumper, with extremely expensive tastes in all areas but little appreciation of how it was all funded. Both Harriet and Vanessa were passionate about Cresswell...but did Rupert, he often wondered, understand this trait in his future bride?

And there was Clare, his paternal aunt. He was very fond of Clare, despite her sometimes daffy ways, but even she had a very expensive hobby. She collected paintings and antique porcelain.

They all, with the possible exception of Lord Weaver, had very decided ideas.

He got up and went over to the mantelpiece. There was a framed photo of himself on it staring out over a vast, untamed landscape. He studied it for a long moment. It epitomised the call of the wild he'd had to resist for the last five years, which he'd spent nurturing the Hocking empire and his mother, aunt and sister. Then he turned away and dragged his thoughts back to his sister's wedding.

'Here's hoping you have a solid constitution, Chas Bartlett, wedding consultant,' he said to himself. 'What you really need to be is a battering ram in a velvet glove.'

*   *   *

Charity Bartlett, nicknamed Chas from childhood, did not tend to make the people who knew her think of her in 'solid' or 'battering ram' terms, even within a velvet glove.

She was twenty-six, with deep blue eyes, pale skin and a mass of rich brown shoulder-length hair with a slight kink in it. She was five feet four, leggy and slender, with narrow hands and feet.

One did discover, if you got to know her, that she was warm and friendly, extremely active and energetic. She was a good lateral thinker but she had trouble telling her left hand from her right without the large round gold watch on a sturdy leather band, which she always wore, and possessed a poor sense of direction.

None of this interfered with her sheer artistry in putting together that 'one perfect day'. She credited her parents' genes for this. Her father, a cordon bleu chef, owned and ran a gourmet delicatessen and extremely 'in' café. Her mother, Hope, the head buyer for a chain of fashion stores, travelled overseas twice a year and was *au fait* with all the latest fashions. *Her* mother, Chas's grandmother, Faith, had owned an antique shop and taken interior-design commissions. For as long as she could remember, Chas had been exposed to wonderful food, elegant clothes and lovely homes.

Since her father and grandmother could also be classified as highly excitable people, it was her mother who must have passed on to Chas some practical genes. It was these genes, added to her innate sense of style, that had enabled Chas to build up a wedding-consultancy business and make a go of it.

She'd called her consultancy The Perfect Day and ran it from her apartment in Brisbane. Thanks to the Richmond-Dailey wedding in Toowoomba, eighty miles west of Brisbane, Chas's reputation had spread, she discovered as she took a call from one Birdie Tait, on behalf of someone called Thomas Hocking.

'May I speak to Chas Bartlett?' Birdie said down the line.

'Speaking,' Chas replied.

'But—is this The Perfect Day wedding consultancy?'

'Yes, it is, and I am Chas Bartlett, which is a bit confusing, I know. Chas is actually short for Charity.'

'I see,' Birdie said slowly.

'Is that a problem, me not being a man—uh—Ms Tait?'

'Well, no.' Birdie sounded a bit confused, however. 'It's just that Laura Richmond gave me to understand—the thing is, she only ever mentioned you by name, not by gender, now I come to think of it, so...' She trailed off.

Chas looked heavenwards. The Richmond-Dailey wedding had been a nightmare to organize, thanks to the bride's mother, whom Chas had privately nicknamed Attila the Hen. Yet now it sounded as if Laura might have recommended her to someone.

You're a genius, kid! Chas complimented herself with a grin.

'Well,' Birdie said again, 'would you be interested in organising another wedding on the Darling Downs, Ms Bartlett?'

Ten minutes later Chas put the phone down and studied the notes she'd made.

Cresswell Lodge, the Hocking family, a peer of the realm—no, the son of a peer of the realm, but still a lord. Lord Weaver to be exact.

Chas stopped reading her notes at this point and got up to waltz around her studio. You beauty!

When Birdie Tait put down her phone, she studied it unseeingly for a long moment, then she shrugged.

Tom had found the idea of a man organising Vanessa's wedding surprising, so he was not likely to take issue with Chas Bartlett being a woman, was he?

She had sounded rather young, though. Still, anyone who'd survived Laura Richmond must be quite tough, so why was she, Birdie, worried?

It came to her. Surviving Laura Richmond and surviving Tom Hocking were two entirely different matters…

Birdie bit her lip. But sounding young didn't necessarily mean you *were* young and impressionable in that regard, did it? All the same, for all concerned, it would probably be a good thing if Chas Bartlett wasn't young, impressionable—and pretty.

She pulled the phone towards her again and rang the stud but all she got was the answering machine. She left a message for Tom, telling him it was all set up for next Saturday and correcting her mistaken information on the wedding consultant's sex.

Then she tried his mobile but it was unattended so she left a short message saying that Miss Charity Bartlett was arriving on Saturday, and asking him to either call her or check his emails. She then posted him an email message.

More, other than take to carrier pigeons, she thought exasperatedly, I cannot do.

Once she'd started to make money, Chas had invested in a royal-blue Range Rover. She'd had the back seat taken out so there was plenty of space for samples, dress boxes, boxes of invitations and the like.

It was a clear Saturday afternoon as she drove west of Brisbane and via Cunningham's Gap towards Gladfield, the address of Cresswell Lodge.

The flat-topped vertical striations of the Great Dividing Range stood out rocky, grand and tinged with blue in the clear air. The bellbirds were calling as she drove through the Gap.

On the top of the range, the scenery changed to mostly flat and the temperature dropped a bit. It was early spring so the landscape of vast paddocks was still tending towards dry and old gold or raw and ploughed.

She'd been told to arrive around four and she was running on time. To help with her often non-existent sense of direction, she'd got detailed instructions from Birdie and drawn herself a large-scale map in thick black felt-tip pen.

She turned off the highway as instructed and took a few back roads through the paddocks. She turned right into Cresswell Lane and it ended at the gates of the lodge. Pretty impressive gates too, with horses rampant on each gatepost.

Horses, Chas thought, and—carriages. I haven't done a horse and carriage wedding yet but this mob might be perfect for it!

She drove on between well-fenced paddocks, past a lovely old barn with a central cupola, then the drive climbed a bit and as she breasted the rise she took a quick, excited breath. Cresswell Lodge homestead was a gem as it spread out below.

Beneath a vast green roof, the walls were of honey-coloured stone. The house was L-shaped with paved verandas. Some of the walls and posts were creeper-hung, and a smooth lawn flowed down to a creek flanked by graceful old willow trees.

Curls of smoke were coming from the chimneys and two dogs were gambolling on the lawn—a large Great Dane and a miniature fox terrier. They stopped gambolling and streaked towards the Range Rover as she pulled to a stop.

A woman in her sixties, all kitted out in riding gear, came round the corner of the house and called the dogs to order as Chas got out of the car. They took no notice of her.

'Hello! Who are you? Don't worry about Leroy and Piccanin, they don't bite.'

Since Leroy, who had to be the Great Dane, now had his paws on her shoulders and had her pinned to the car as he licked her face, this was just as well, Chas felt.

'Um—down boy!' She wiped her face with her jacket sleeve. 'I'm Chas Bartlett. I believe I'm expected.'

'Good heavens! We thought you were a man! How do you do? I'm Harriet Hocking, Vanessa's mother. To be perfectly honest, I'm relieved. I was expecting some long-haired arty chap.'

'You were? But—uh—Ms Tait knew I wasn't a man, after the initial confusion.'

Harriet raised her eyebrows. She was good-looking, thanks to great bone structure and a slim figure, but in a rather weathered kind of no-nonsense way. 'Well, she somehow failed to pass it on; not like our Birdie. Never mind, come in!'

Several exhausting hours later, Chas closed herself into her bedroom, slipped her shoes off and sat down on the bed.

Then she lay back flat across the bed with her arms outstretched and started to laugh softly. Beside Harriet, Vanessa and Clare Hocking, Laura Richmond paled into insignificance.

If she could get this wedding to the altar she'd be more than a genius!

She sat up. The only member of the immediate wedding party not present this evening had been the man who had hired her, Thomas Hocking. Would it be too much to hope that he might actually be normal?

Yes, it would, she decided.

She herself had brought his name up halfway through dinner—a dinner that she would probably remember for a long time. It had been served in a large panelled room at a vast table with silver cutlery, crystal glasses and Wedgwood china. A pale, tense-looking young man, apparently part of the kitchen staff, had dished up and passed around a feast.

'I thought Thomas Hocking might be here since he actually hired me, I believe,' she ventured at the dessert stage—brandy pudding and custard, which she was secretly viewing with despair after all the food that had gone before.

'Thomas?' Vanessa, a stunning brunette, raised her eyebrows and smirked. 'As a matter of fact, *Thomas* more or less press-ganged the rest of us into being here, then he sloped off. Typical, and with a woman, no doubt! I bet it's that peachy blonde who's opened up a riding school down the road.'

'She certainly finds plenty of opportunities to visit Cresswell,' Harriet said drily, 'so you can't exactly blame Thomas.'

'Can't you?' Vanessa said with some patent cynicism. 'If there wasn't such a very long line of them, I might agree.' She shrugged and turned to Chas. 'Don't worry about it,' she advised. 'He's only paying for the wedding.'

'If the details were left to him,' Harriet said, 'Vanessa would have to make do with a registry office, come to that.'

Clare Hocking, about the same age as her sister-in-law, Harriet, put in, 'There is a lot to be said for elegant simplicity, you know.'

They all gazed at her. Far from elegantly simple in her appearance, Clare wore several layers of clothing, none of which matched, as well as a stole and three long necklaces. Her silvery hair was tumbling out of a bun and she had two bright spots of artificial colour on each cheek, rather like a clown.

'All the same…' Rupert, Lord Weaver, cleared his throat. 'I'm quite sure we won't have to r-resort to a r-registry office. He would never do that to you, Vannie,' he added reproachfully.

'However, he can,' Harriet said at large, 'make things awkward, as we all know. Therefore this way, with Chas here to help—*at his suggestion*—we can keep the rest of his involvement to a minimum.'

'Agreed.' Vanessa pushed away her dessert plate and reached for a plum. 'So whatever you do, Chas, take a stern line with Thomas!'

A womaniser, obviously, Chas thought as she considered Thomas Hocking in the privacy of her bedroom, but who was he and what other bizarre qualities did he possess?

He obviously held the purse strings but he didn't

sound like Vanessa's father or Harriet's husband. An uncle perhaps, who was now the head of the family? Who was resented, even, not only for his grip on those purse strings but also for his reprehensible taste in peachy young blondes?

She shook her head. Time would tell. In the meantime, the couple of hours after dinner she'd spent with Vanessa, Harriet and Clare had been tricky to say the least.

She'd listened to Vanessa's ideas for her wedding and her dress, she'd listened to both Harriet and Clare's ideas, and had formed the opinion that never would the trio meet.

That was when she'd quietly produced her folder of wedding dresses and pointed to the one she felt would suit Vanessa best.

There'd been a startled silence, then Vanessa had jumped up and thrown her arms around Chas. 'It's perfect! So different but so beautiful.'

'It is lovely,' Harriet agreed.

'My, my!' Clare enthused.

Then they discussed venues, and Chas gave her opinion that Cresswell Lodge was the perfect spot for a wedding reception. And, thinking rapidly, she outlined some ideas for decorating the house and garden for a wedding, including a silk-lined marquee on the lawn, because, as she told them, she never took chances with the weather.

'Ah,' Harriet said thoughtfully, 'not just a pretty face, Chas Bartlett.'

'I hope not, Mrs Hocking,' Chas replied. 'I did also wonder if it mightn't be appropriate for the bride and groom to arrive at the reception in a horse-drawn carriage. Naturally they'd have to drive from the church

in Warwick by car, but we could do a discreet change-
over somehow or other. And horses do seem to feature
prominently in your lives.'

Harriet sat up and Vanessa drew an excited breath.
'Awesome!' she said.

'Wonderful,' Harriet agreed. 'You can leave that bit
to me, Chas. Of course, we'd need matching carriage
horses but that shouldn't be too hard.'

Chas came back to the present and bit her lip. Matching
horses?

She really needed to know what her budget would
be before she made any more expensive suggestions.
Not—she gazed around the impressive guest bedroom—that the Hockings appeared to be short of a
dime, but there was the mysterious Thomas and his
'registry office' notions to take into account.

She yawned and was startled to see it was close to
midnight so she changed into her night gear. Then she
remembered that, impressive though the room was,
with a king-size bed invitingly turned down, lovely
drapes and a matching carpet, and warm as it was from
central heating, there was no *en suite* bathroom.

The guest bathroom was several doors down a passage. She picked up her sponge bag and walked to the
door, and the lights flickered, went out and stayed out.

Damn, she thought. I *hate* going to bed without
cleaning my teeth! I'll just have to manage in the dark.

She stepped out into the passage and waited a few
moments for her eyes to adjust to the gloom. The house
was quite silent.

She found the bathroom and, after a bit of fumbling
around, managed to clean her teeth, wash her face and
attend to all else that was necessary.

As she came out of the bathroom she hesitated and felt for her watch. It wasn't there, for the simple reason that she'd taken it off when she was changing.

Not that it matters, she assured herself. I know that I have to turn this way, count two doors down and the third is my bedroom.

It all worked to plan and with a sigh of relief she shut herself into the room. There was nothing for it but to go to bed, since the lights were still out—she'd flicked the switch she'd groped for beside the door then flicked it off when nothing had happened. She pulled off her robe, felt around for the bed, and slipped into it.

The next few moments were electrifying. An arm descended on her waist, a sleepy exclamation issued forth, a pair of hands started to run down her body and a man's deep voice said, 'Holy mackerel! Not again!'

CHAPTER TWO

CHAS gasped, twisted and reared up. To her mortification, the sounds she uttered, which were meant to be serious screams, came out instead as a series of squeaks.

'Whoa!' She was determinedly wrestled back to the bed. 'Look here, sweetheart, you came into my bed, not the other way around, so your objections are a bit bogus, surely?'

'Stop!' Chas hissed.

'Why? Do I know you?'

'No! There's been a terrible mistake.'

To her fury, he moved his hands on her again, from her breasts down to her waist, and left them there. 'Mistake?' he mused as his hands almost spanned her waist. 'I would have thought you were rather divinely put together, Aphrodite. Definitely an ornament to any man's bed.'

'Will you stop doing that!' Chas commanded as she wriggled beneath the feel of his hands on her body. Not that he was hurting her. It was the opposite if anything...

'I can explain. I must have lost—' she stopped as the bedside lamp flickered on '—my way,' she finished as her eyes widened.

She was in another vast bed but this one had a magnificent carved headboard. The pillows were plump and exotic, the colours ranging from pomegranate to slate-blue, and there were at least six of them. The sheets were slate and the quilt, now pushed aside, was patterned in pomegranate on a slate background.

Two bedside tables carved to match the bedhead bore lamps with silver foil shades. The walls were mushroom-pink, the ceiling was *café au lait* and a vast expanse of pale-toffee carpet fled into the shadows.

It was a stunning bedroom but not only that. Talk about Aphrodite—she was in the hands of a stranger who could have been Adonis.

The silence stretched as they stared at each other.

He had longish brown hair and a broad forehead tapering to a determined chin. He had smoky grey eyes, highly quizzical but all the same quite magnetic, beneath darker brows. He was naked, to the waist at least, and just about male perfection personified.

The skin of his broad shoulders was smooth and golden. His chest was sleekly muscled and sprinkled with dark hair, his throat was strong and his hands, now removed from her body, were tapered but powerful.

If she was taken aback, so was he, for a moment, as his grey gaze roamed over her.

He inspected her mass of shiny dark hair, the oval of her face, the naked pink of her lips and the velvet blue of her eyes.

She wore a slip of a cranberry silk nightgown with shoestring straps. It had a V-neckline that plunged quite low and the creamy swell of her breasts was visible. The narrowness of her waist was hinted at and the lovely curve of her hips was more than hinted at where the cranberry silk clung. Her legs were long and slender and her skin was satiny.

He took it all in then returned his gaze to hers, and as their eyes locked, for one crazy moment, Chas felt as if she'd all along been destined for this bed and this man; it just seemed—fitting somehow.

Her lips parted in amazement as the kind of *frisson* she hadn't experienced for a while touched her deliciously in all her secret places down her smooth body.

He read the amazement in her eyes and the ghost of a smile touched his mouth, then he looked down her body again.

The nightgown ended just below her hips and was rucked up anyway.

She followed his gaze down to her thighs and, with a gasp of horror, pulled the sheet up to her throat.

He smiled lazily this time and said softly, 'Closing the stable door after the horse has bolted, Aphrodite? You really are a mass of contradictions.'

Chas sat bolt upright, still clutching the sheet with some hazy idea of wrapping herself in it while she beat a hasty retreat, but he anchored his side of it firmly to the bed. He also circled his other hand round one of her wrists.

'What are you doing?' Her eyes widened.

'Taking out some insurance,' he drawled. 'Just in case you decide to rush from the room screaming rape.'

'I had no intention of doing that!'

He shrugged. 'Ah, seduction then. Tell you what, I'll make up my mind about that in a moment. So,' he said, 'you lost your way?'

Chas felt a tremor of fear run through her—what had she got herself into? She set her teeth. 'Yes. There was a power failure. I—I went to the bathroom and got…disorientated.'

'Really?'

There was so much sardonic disbelief in this single word that Chas blushed vividly, but she soldiered on.

'If you don't believe me, how do you explain your lamp coming on of its own accord?'

He thought for a moment. 'I decided to read for a while.' He reached around and pulled a book from under a pillow. 'I must have fallen asleep with the lamp on, and we do get power failures. That would explain—some things,' he said and sat up suddenly, although he didn't release her wrist. 'Who are you?' he asked grimly.

'I—I'm here to organise a wedding,' she said disjointedly, 'but I'm having some trouble convincing myself this isn't a madhouse.'

His eyebrows disappeared into his hair. 'Chas Bartlett in drag?' he queried incredulously, his gaze resting on her breasts again. 'Or, no. Would you be his assistant, perhaps? Sent to secure the deal in the time-honoured way?'

She stared at him with her mouth open.

'Don't play the innocent with me,' he advised softly. 'It happens. So what exactly does The Perfect Day wedding consultancy supply? Your services in my bed as well?'

Chas drew a deep breath into her lungs and swung her free hand so that it connected with his cheek, hard.

He didn't even flinch, but jerked her into his arms. 'If that's how you like it, rough, two can play that game,' he said barely audibly.

His arms felt like iron bars around her. The look in his eyes, of serious contempt, frightened the life out of her but what was even more frightening was the realisation that, contemptuous or not, he intended to kiss her...

'Don't, don't—don't!' she warned.

'Don't kiss you? Why not? You may have an avaricious little soul but your body is another matter.' He loosened his arms slightly and looked downwards. 'Another matter entirely.'

Chas twisted like an eel and managed to free herself, but only momentarily. She was just about to slip off the bed when he caught her wrist again. 'Oh, no, you don't, sweetheart,' he drawled. 'We haven't finished what you started yet.'

She was breathing tumultuously. 'L-look—I mean, l-listen to me,' she stammered. 'I *am* Chas Bartlett. It's short for Charity. There's only me in the wedding consultancy—you've got it all wrong. And I did lose my way! What's more, if you lay another finger on me I will scream rape and blue murder.'

A little silence developed as they faced each other. He was still holding her wrist but he pushed himself up on his elbow and studied her. Her hair was gloriously disarrayed, she was flushed and still breathing heavily, but her blue eyes were deadly serious.

He rubbed his knuckles along his jaw and pulled the sheet up.

'So you were a woman all along?' He frowned. 'Why did Birdie think you were a man?'

'People assume Chas is short for Charles.'

'What's wrong with Charity?' he queried.

'Nothing, unless your grandmother is Faith and your mother Hope. I think I was about nine when I decided that Charity was a bit much.' She stopped and eyed him with extreme frustration. 'What's that got to do with anything? I'm quite sure this is a madhouse now. And who the hell are you?'

'I just happen to live here.' He smiled fleetingly. 'What makes you think this is a madhouse? I mean...' he shrugged those magnificent shoulders '...I'm tempted to agree with you at times, but how would you know?'

Chas sent him a smouldering look. 'I'll tell you. I was hired by someone called Thomas Hocking, who brought me all this way specifically so he could meet me, then didn't even have the decency to turn up to-night, apparently because according to his own family he's too busy womanising. And now I'm told that he, the man paying for the wedding, would much rather have a registry-office do!' This time her eyes flashed scornfully. 'That's not the kind of wedding I put to-gether, and it makes me wonder why I'm here and if he can afford me. It just doesn't make sense.'

'Oh, he could.'

Chas blinked a couple of times as she tried to put this in context. 'He could what?'

'Afford you.'

The way he said it caused Chas to stir uneasily. 'I meant afford my services, naturally,' she said.

'That too.' His grey gaze rested on her mouth.

'What—? Are we talking about the same thing?'

His lips twisted. 'I don't think so. I happen to know Thomas Hocking is—how to put it—between mis-tresses at the moment, and I've got the distinct feeling he'd be very happy to afford you in that capacity.'

'Let me go!' Chas said furiously and struggled to free herself.

All she achieved was to lose control of her side of the sheet as he swept it aside, although his action did at least reveal that he was wearing a pair of sleep shorts. At the same time it left her completely exposed to him again, and he made the best of it.

'Mmm…' he murmured, studying her from head to toe and all the curves, the expanse of pale, skimpilydraped-with-cranberry-silk skin, in between. 'Love the legs. Definitely mistress material.'

'Who…who are you?' she stammered as she tugged her nightgown down as far as she could.

'Tom Hocking, ma'am. No one calls me Thomas, except Birdie.'

Chas gasped as all sorts of things fell into place. One of them being her sheer stupidity. Who else but the man controlling the purse strings would have what definitely looked like the master bedroom? Why hadn't she thought of that? Because she'd had a mental vision of an elderly profligate uncle or something! Which was not to say that this Thomas Hocking wasn't profligate. His intentions only minutes earlier would have certainly fallen into that category.

'Of all the…' she said with deep outrage. 'How could you do this?'

'Do what? Fall asleep peacefully in my own bed, on my own, until you climbed into it? That's all I recall.'

Her breasts heaved. 'No it's not! You misrepresented yourself, you won't believe me and you're keeping me here against my will!'

He opened his mouth then appeared to change his mind. 'If you got to the bathroom safely, how come you ended up here?'

Chas winced. 'It is a strange house, and with no lights it's not so surprising. Anyway, I don't have a great sense of direction and I didn't have my watch on.'

He stared at her. 'Would that have helped? What is it? A luminous compass as well as a watch? A miniature GPS?'

'Very funny,' Chas said stiffly. 'No, but it does help me tell my right hand from my left.'

'You got to your—mid-twenties,' he hazarded, 'without being able to tell your right from your left? That certainly explains it.'

Chas set her teeth at the irony in his eyes. 'It can happen, believe me.'

He looked as if he wanted to say *you learn something every day!*, and ruffled his hair. 'Well, where do we go from here, Aphrodite?'

'So *no one* calls you Thomas?'

'I can't remember the last time anyone did, apart from Birdie. Why?'

Chas wrenched her wrist free and tumbled off the bed. 'Where do we go? Back to Brisbane first thing, for me at least. I don't appreciate being made a fool of like this!' She grabbed her robe and sponge bag and ran from the room.

Breakfast was a help-yourself affair.

Juice and coffee were set on a buffet table as well as cereals, yoghurt, fruit and a frosted jug of milk. Several silver-lidded warming dishes were lined up and there was a basket of rolls and bread.

The only person in the dining room when Chas entered was Rupert. There was one word that summed up Rupert Leeton, Lord Weaver, and that was diffident. He wasn't particularly good-looking, he was of medium height, he could most easily disappear in a crowd but, despite his obvious reticence, he was nice.

A good match for Vanessa Hocking? Chas had wondered. Perhaps only time would tell.

She'd calmed down somewhat since her encounter with Tom Hocking but she wasn't feeling particularly charitable towards any of the Cresswell Lodge inhabitants, so she murmured a cool greeting.

Rupert, however, rose courteously to pull out a chair for her and offered to fetch her a glass of juice.

'Thank you.'

'As a matter of fact I feel like saying that to you!' Rupert placed a glass of orange juice in front of her. 'Vanessa's like a new person since your session last night. They were getting all bogged down and it was definitely getting on Tom's nerves,' he confided. 'But your ideas have breathed new life into the old girl!'

'Ah, Tom,' Chas murmured, and flicked the bridegroom a reproachful glance.

'Of course!' He tapped his forehead. 'You have no idea who Tom is, do you?'

'She does now.'

Chas froze as Tom Hocking strolled into the room and poured himself a cup of coffee at the buffet. He sat down opposite Chas with it. 'Don't you, Ms Bartlett?' he added.

Chas swallowed. 'Yes.'

Tom Hocking smiled and turned to Rupert. 'What's this you've been telling her about me being a womaniser, as well as all sorts of weird things?'

Rupert grimaced and attempted several garbled explanations. 'It was the *Thomas* that did it,' he finished. 'It sort of took us by surprise, and then—the girls were just feeling a bit highly strung, I suppose.'

'Is that so?' Tom murmured.

Chas studied him. In contrast to Rupert, who was clean and crisp, Tom Hocking had dark shadows on his jaw. He was in his socks, he wore faded jeans and a stained khaki work shirt but—this surprised her—he was not unimpressive.

'Lord Weaver,' she said coolly, rather than dwelling on the physical properties that made Tom Hocking stand out even in his work clothes, 'didn't start it. He defended you if anything.'

'Thank you, Rupe,' Tom said with obvious irony. He rose, picked up his cup and said to her, 'I'd like to see you in my study when you've finished your breakfast, Ms Bartlett. It might be a good idea to get someone to show you right to the door.'

He strolled out.

Rupert clicked his tongue. 'Sorry about that. It obviously led to a misunderstanding.'

Chas started to say something about a monumental understatement but confined herself to murmuring, 'You could say so. I get the feeling he's not an easy person to handle at the best of times, however.'

Rupert considered and shrugged. 'He does have the final say around here. He is very successful.'

'Perhaps he needs more than a cup of coffee for breakfast?' she suggested with a tinge of frivolity she was far from feeling.

'Oh, he would have been up and about hours ago. He always breakfasts first then goes out to the horses.'

'I see. One of those?'

Rupert smiled. 'In a word.'

Chas finished her breakfast but not with great enjoyment. Then she made a point of cleaning her teeth before asking her way to Tom Hocking's study.

He was on the phone to, it emerged, Birdie Tait. He waved her to a chair and continued his conversation, giving Chas ample time to look around. Like the dining room the study was panelled and, like the rest of the house, was beautifully furnished with antiques—a marvellous old oak desk, two winged chairs with linen covers and a lovely array of art on the walls.

So impressed by the art was she, she got up to have a closer look and didn't realise he'd finished his phone call until he said her name.

'Oh!' She moved back to the chair and sank into it.

They stared at each other across the desk for a long moment.

He was now showered and shaved and wore khaki trousers and a blue sweater with military-style patches on the elbows and shoulders. Unfortunately, Chas discovered, these clothes did not prevent her from seeing him in her mind's eye wearing nothing but a pair of sleep shorts.

To her further confusion, from the light of pure devilry in his grey eyes, she had no doubt that his mind's eye had swept away her blue jeans and apricot jumper and he was seeing her in only a flimsy slip of a nightgown.

She prayed that she wouldn't blush but she did, and it got worse than that. Her nipples tingled, causing her to move abruptly.

There was no way he could have known this had happened to her, not beneath a bra and jumper, but she got the feeling, as his eyes narrowed, that he did. Her awkward movement must have given her away.

'Yes, well,' he drawled, 'you remind me of a long-legged, skittish filly, but what have you to say for yourself this morning, Ms Bartlett?'

Chas drew on all the composure she possessed and remembered her determination to eschew all mention of the events in his bed. 'I don't think this is a very good idea, Mr Hocking,' she said briskly. 'I don't believe we could work together, so—'

'It's my sister and my mother you'd be working with,' he interrupted. 'Incidentally, Birdie has cleared up a lot of the confusion. Apparently she left all sorts of messages for me regarding your metamorphosis into a woman that I never got.'

'Never got?' Chas frowned.

'You will find, should you accept this commission, that it helps to be a horse around here.' This time he studied her hair caught back at the nape of her neck.

Chas blinked.

'Yes,' he continued, 'all the best treatment is re-served for the horses. Other things, like answering machines, mobile-phone messages and the like get short shrift. Someone borrowed my mobile phone; someone accidentally deleted the message tape on the answering machine. I must admit, I just forgot to check my emails. Birdie is at her wits' end with us.'

Chas shrugged. 'I'm not surprised. But that actually makes me more sure that this would be an impossible wedding to organise, Mr Hocking, and—'

'Why? You appear to have slayed my mother and my sister with your ideas.'

Chas hesitated. 'That's the other thing. They did lead me to believe you—uh—might not appreciate the costs involved.'

He smiled somewhat grimly and named a figure.

Chas's eyes widened and her lips parted.

'That obviously surprises you, Ms Bartlett. Not enough?'

'Plenty,' Chas said, then bit her lip.

He lay back in his chair. 'I may run a tight ship, which they like to interpret, occasionally, as me being cheap, but I wouldn't expect Vanessa to marry Lord Weaver without all the trimmings.'

Chas was lost for words.

'Look…' He sat forward. 'I apologise for everything

that led up to you feeling you'd been made a fool of last night. But it was me they were taking the mickey out of, not you.'

'And you didn't feel you were making fun of me when—?' She stopped exasperatedly on the thought that she hadn't planned to mention that.

'When I was…? Talking about mistress material?' he suggested. 'Actually—' his eyes glinted '—I was serious, and that was a compliment.'

'Well, that depends entirely, Mr Hocking,' Chas said, 'on your reputation with women. Was your family maligning you there, do you feel?'

'I don't know what they said.' He still looked amused.

'That you'd sloped off last night, with a woman, no doubt,' she elucidated.

His amusement changed to injury. 'I did not! Well, I guess there was a female involved, actually. Two, as it happens.'

Pure blue scorn beamed his way.

'I was called out, Ms Bartlett,' he continued, 'to help with a difficult foaling. Both the dam and a filly foal survived and are doing well now.'

For a moment Chas wished she could fall through the floor. 'So…so why did they say that?'

He shrugged. 'I may have forgotten to mention it to anyone.' He waited for a moment then said softly, 'Don't you have a sense of humour, Chas?'

'I have a very well-developed sense of humour normally,' she said slowly. 'Climbing into a strange man's bed seems to have dampened it somewhat.'

'Why don't we start again?'

She swallowed.

'You may have carte blanche within the limits of

your budget. I don't know if anyone's mentioned this but Rupert's parents, the Earl and Countess of Wickham, will be attending. So will several other lords and ladies. I'm quite sure this wedding will find its way into some English magazines and papers, not to mention Australian ones.'

Chas clicked her tongue. 'That's blackmail.'

He said nothing.

'But I do run a business,' she added a little helplessly.

He nodded in serious agreement.

'Oh, all right!' Chas was goaded into flinging at him.

He sat back and made a steeple of his fingers. 'I thought it might be.'

'Look here, if you're as successful as they say you are, why take exception to my commercial instincts?' Chas challenged.

'I'm not. It's your other instincts I'm wondering about.'

'Such as?'

'How much…' He paused thoughtfully. 'How much of your decision was based on curiosity? A mutual curiosity, I do admit, but one stemming from your inability to tell your left hand from your right last night?'

Chas rose. 'None whatsoever! I happen to be the ultimate career girl.'

'Who said anything about interfering—' his gaze drifted down her figure '—with your career?'

'I'm saying it now. I never mix business with pleasure, Mr Hocking—not that I would classify you as pleasure—and I have no intention of joining a long line of peachy blondes!'

He looked askance at her. 'Peachy blondes?'

'That was the other detail your family imparted last

night. Peachy blondes, such as the riding-school owner who has supposedly taken to haunting this place.'

He opened his mouth to reply but she turned on her heel and walked out.

He said, just before she reached the door, 'If you'd left your hair loose you could have tossed your head just like an exasperated filly.'

She stayed on for the morning but declined lunch.

She also managed to detach Vanessa from her mother and aunt. And she had the felicity, when she said to Vanessa that above all it was her wedding and the important choices should all be *hers*, of being spontaneously and gratefully hugged.

They chose the invitations, decided on the bridesmaids' dresses—there were to be two plus a flower-girl and a page-boy—and what the men of the wedding party would wear. Vanessa selected a colour scheme for the decorations and flowers. They discussed menus and looked through a selection of wedding cakes, and Vanessa promised to send Chas a guest list so the invitations could go out.

At the end of the session, Vanessa looked Chas over curiously. 'I could never have sorted this all out on my own. I could never have made up my mind! How do you do it?'

Chas grinned. 'I'm not sure. Perhaps it's because I love weddings and I love seeing them being the happy, joyful occasions they should be.'

'Ever had one of your own?'

Chas hesitated. 'Funnily enough, almost. Then he— We decided to call it off.'

'Wouldn't that turn you off weddings for life?' Vanessa queried.

'Oh, I was already in the business but—no,' Chas said slowly and with a faint frown, 'it didn't.'

'Did it turn you off men?'

'Ah!' Chas looked humorous. 'That's another matter. Dashing, very good-looking men who get away with murder, perhaps. And I'm certainly not into serious relationships now.'

She gathered together all her papers and returned to business. 'Vanessa, we only have three months, which isn't a great deal of time for a wedding this size, but if you want to change anything, do let me know. By the way, who is giving you away?'

'Tom.' Vanessa grimaced. 'With unconcealed relief, no doubt—no, that's not fair.' She got up and looked out of the window over the garden. 'We may joke about it and get mad with him sometimes, but without Tom we'd be lost.' She turned back to Chas abruptly. 'Do you know how much I love this place?'

Chas blinked. 'No. I mean, so would most people probably.'

'It's part of me,' Vanessa said slowly, then changed the subject again. 'You will come up often, won't you?'

'Of course, as often as I can.'

Chas drove home in a slightly better frame of mind than the one she'd started the day in, but she found she had Vanessa Hocking on her mind.

A strange mixture, she thought. Those arrogant Hocking airs her brother could turn on in spades—she broke off and shivered as she recalled the way Tom Hocking had looked at her from time to time—but then a glimpse of vulnerability in Vanessa, which was certainly not in Tom.

*   *   *

The next morning, Monday, she began to make arrangements for the Weaver-Hocking wedding. She engaged caterers, she hired the marquee as well as chairs and tables. She got in touch with her favourite florist and a hairdresser who also did make-up.

It was a slight tussle on account of lack of time to persuade the wedding-dress specialists whose work she really admired to take on the creation of the wedding and bridesmaids' dresses, until she mentioned that the groom was heir to a peer of the realm. It produced an instant response—not only would they be happy to do the dresses, but they'd also be happy to travel to Gladfield to take measurements and for future fittings.

She put the phone down with a sigh of relief. That had to be so much easier than co-ordinating Vanessa and the bridesmaids to come down to Brisbane.

She remembered then that one thing they hadn't discussed was music, for the church or the reception, and she made a note to speak to Vanessa about it.

Her next call was to her mother about Harriet and Clare's outfits plus the bride's trousseau.

'The thing is,' she said down the phone, 'I'm a little short of time for getting the outfits for the mother and aunt of the bride designed and made, but I'm terrified that if they're off the rack, someone else will turn up at the wedding in them.'

'Come and see me at work, darling,' Hope Bartlett advised. 'We're thinking of featuring a new designer, she's very good and very keen to make her mark. She might well consider a wedding commission, especially a wedding like this—didn't you say the bridegroom was a lord? Worth her while, despite the short notice. And I can certainly help you out with the trousseau.'

'You're a pet, Mum! And what would I do without Rupert?'

'Come again?'

'He's the lord, Rupert Leeton, Lord Weaver. You have no idea what doors that name unlocks!'

On Tuesday, Chas drove down to the Gold Coast for a conference with staff of the luxury hotel where one of her other weddings was to be staged in the ballroom.

At the end of a satisfying talk, she strolled out into the beautiful gardens that gave onto the beach to pick out the optimum spot for the wedding photos.

The last person she expected to bump into was Tom Hocking.

CHAPTER THREE

'THE wedding consultant, alias Aphrodite,' he said and paused. 'But looking as if she needs a handy hole to fall down.'

Chas regained some of her composure. Ignore the Aphrodite reference, she told herself firmly. He'll only trip me up with it, make me blush or worse. 'If I'm—surprised, it's because you're the last person I expected to see.'

'Or the last person on the planet you'd like to see?' he mused. 'Is that what you really mean?'

She shrugged. 'You choose, Mr Hocking. What does bring you here? *I*,' she supplied conversationally, 'am here on business, wedding business.'

He stood and looked at her for a moment.

There was little resemblance to the master of Cresswell Stud in his attire of navy trousers and a pale blue linen shirt that could have been Armani. His black leather shoes and belt looked to be hand-stitched, and his brown hair was smooth and sleek.

Mind you, her mental processes told Chas, none of it hid the ruggedly elegant frame beneath his clothes. None of it changed the disturbing power of that grey gaze as it rested on her thoughtfully.

In fact, she was even prompted to wonder whether she and Tom Hocking would ever be able to be in each other's company without the fateful memory of those minutes together in his bed coming between them.

He certainly took his time about his appraisal of her.

She wore three-quarter hot-pink trousers and a white T-shirt beneath a burnt-orange short-sleeved jacket. Her high sandals matched her jacket and her patent bag matched the trousers. It was a chic, colourful outfit and she had a heavy gold bracelet on her right hand. Her hair was loose and riotous. Despite a fairly intense conference with the hotel staff, she looked as fresh as a daisy.

'Mmm…' he said at last, but whether it was approval or not, Chas had no idea. 'Uh—I'm staying here. I have one or two people to see, and a business deal to close. Let me buy you a drink, Ms Bartlett.'

'Oh, there's no need for that. I mean, thank you,' Chas rephrased, 'but I do have to drive back to Brisbane.'

'What about an iced coffee, then?' He turned to a passing waiter and placed the order for two iced coffees. 'How about that table over there?' he suggested to Chas. 'Under the umbrella.'

Chas contemplated telling him he was the absolute limit, but he took advantage of the pause to stroll over to the table and pull out a chair for her.

Short of making a scene, there wasn't much she could do but take her seat.

'This is nice,' he said, and gestured to the view of the sea beyond the gardens.

'It is,' she agreed, 'although that's hardly the point. Never mind, perhaps we can talk business,' she added, and began, detail by minute detail, to advise him of the arrangements she'd put in place for his sister's wedding, until he laughed and put up a hand in defence.

'No more, please, Chas, you're making me dizzy.'

'I just thought you might like to know how I'm spending your money,' she replied innocently.

'Rather than paying me back for calling you Aphrodite? Of course.' He paused as their coffees were served, then he asked the waiter to pass on to Reception where he was, since he was expecting some guests.

'Certainly, Mr Hocking, sir,' the waiter said deferentially.

The silence between them lengthened after the waiter's departure.

'What?' Tom Hocking said at last.

Chas shook her head. 'I don't know. There's something about you that—' She stopped and gestured with both hands.

'Annoys you?' he suggested.

'So it would seem.' Chas spooned some of the swirled cream atop the iced coffee into her mouth.

'It's probably because of how we met.' His eyes were full of satanic amusement.

'I know that,' she murmured, and flinched as his bedroom returned to her mind's eye.

'Do you really have trouble telling your right from your left, Chas?'

'I really do,' she replied, and felt automatically for her watch. 'Whether you like to believe it or not,' she added. 'Of course, it's worse in the dark.'

All the same, how could she have been so careless? she wondered. And how was she going to cope with continued references to it? Maybe a cool, humorous touch was called for?

'That's a pretty spectacular bedroom you have.' She gestured. 'You could almost say it was designed for seduction.'

He lifted an eyebrow. 'I'm not into "designer" seduction so you'll have to blame the interior decorator my mother got in. No...' He rubbed his knuckles across his jaw and looked at her thoughtfully. 'Come to that, I'm not into seduction at all. I prefer things to be mutually spontaneous. How about you?'

She stared at him frostily and made a mental note to strike all future humorous touches. 'Naturally,' she said, but it didn't sound right, it didn't sound *soignée*, it sounded just like someone who had been bested at her own game. She bit her lip.

He smiled lazily. 'You have a little speck of cream on the corner of your mouth.'

Chas fished her napkin out from below the coffee glass and wiped her mouth.

'That's better,' he drawled then lifted an eyebrow. 'Well, I don't know.'

'What do you mean?' She frowned.

'It's an eminently kissable mouth even without a speck of cream.'

Chas stared at him, her eyes widening and her colour fluctuating.

He started to laugh, with genuine amusement. 'It's OK, that's not a fantasy I'm partial to along with a seduction-guaranteed bedroom. I just couldn't resist it.'

It occurred to Chas that shock, horror and condemnation were becoming all too frequent reactions from her, and could even be fuelling Tom Hocking's desire to shock her. But how to respond otherwise? To her amazement she heard herself having another go at cool amusement.

'I'm glad to hear it,' she said smoothly, 'although there might be plenty of girls willing to *smother* themselves in whipped cream for you—who knows?'

'And you couldn't care less?' he murmured.

'No!' She smiled. 'I'm only the wedding consultant.

Maybe, if I get Vanessa's wedding right, you'll consider me for your own?'

'I doubt it.' He smiled back. 'I think I'd be far better off with someone who didn't remind me of Aphrodite rising out of my bed, I really do.'

'You'd probably need a man, then,' she suggested.

He said softly with those mesmerising grey eyes glinting, 'You're showing your claws, Chas.'

'Don't provoke me.' She looked at him exasperatedly. 'I—' She stopped as three people came up to the table.

'Ah!' Tom rose. 'My guests. Chas, meet Will Darling, Heather, his wife, and Loretta Quinn. This is Chas Bartlett.'

Chas recognised Will Darling immediately. He was a captain of industry seen frequently in the papers and on television. His wealth was legendary; his wife, Heather, was almost as legendary for the parties she gave and an extremely forthright manner.

As for Loretta Quinn, in her late twenties and stunningly beautiful, she played the harp and had just released a solo album that had rocketed to the top of the charts. There was something almost fey about her trademark long, curly fair hair, her pointed little chin and her eyes that were the colour of eucalyptus leaves. She wore all white, a loose, lovely dress with a handkerchief hem.

Both she and Heather Darling kissed Tom with obvious affection before turning to Chas.

'How do you do?' Heather said. 'Are you Tom's new girlfriend? I do hope so. You look rather nice, if you don't mind me saying so.'

'Heather!' Will Darling looked heavenwards, and he

shook Chas's hand. 'Take no notice of her, my dear.
Mind you, she's right about the last bit—Tom?'

'No, although we did meet in bed,' Tom said, and
the absolutely wicked laughter in his eyes caused the
faint pink in Chas's cheeks to deepen. 'Sadly,' he
added as everyone stared at Chas with a kind of fatal
fascination, 'it was by accident. No, she's a wedding
consultant extraordinaire. I hired her for—'

'Not Vanessa's wedding?' Heather broke in excit-
edly. 'Are we talking Vanessa's wedding? I'm so looking forward to it! Has she actually set a date?'

Chas nodded, revealed the date and murmured that
the invitations were due to go out shortly.

'Look here, Will, darling—' Heather turned to her
husband '—don't you dare be anywhere else on that
day! What about you, Loretta?'

Loretta looked injured. 'Would I do that to Vannie?
I promised I'd play the ''Wedding March'' for her.'

Chas took a breath, most of her discomfort melting
at this news. 'That…that would be so lovely!'

'Thanks.' Loretta shrugged.

The conversation became general then and through
it Chas formed the impression that the Darling and the
Hocking families had strong ties, and that Will and
Tom were in together on the business deal that they
hoped to sew up shortly with a Japanese consortium.

Perhaps there was a lot, lot more to the master of
Cresswell than met the eye, she mused at one stage.
Definitely part of the rich and famous, even if he did
go out and help a mare in foaling difficulties…
Although that didn't mean she had to like him.

She made her excuses not long afterwards. Tom
didn't try to detain her and the others of the party said
goodbye with genuine warmth.

She became aware as she walked away that the Darling-Hocking-Quinn gathering was the cynosure of all eyes amongst other guests enjoying the gardens.

It really was the most amazing opportunity for her to break into society weddings, she told herself as she drove home. She'd be mad not to pull out all stops to get this wedding absolutely perfect, with some unique touches.

She stopped at a traffic light, and drummed her fingers on the steering wheel. Does that include a better relationship with the bride's brother? she asked herself. What if he goes on making remarks about how we met? How can I forgive that?

Her parents came round that evening, on their way home from a bargain-basement sale.

Her father collected LPs—his record player was one of the delights of his life—and he'd picked up a box of LPs for a song. He brought them up to show Chas.

'And this,' he said triumphantly, holding a record sleeve aloft, 'I've been trying to track down for years. Herb Alpert. You may not have heard of him, darling, he was well before your time.'

'I don't think anyone who grew up in your house could *not* have heard of Herb Alpert and the Tijuana Brass, Dad,' Chas murmured, 'although I've never seen that.'

'*Whipped Cream and Other Delights*—it came out in 1965,' her father said. 'The cover was quite a talking point.'

'I can imagine.' Chas stared at the stunning dark-haired girl on the cover with a long-stemmed pink rosebud in one hand and wearing a low-cut mantle of whipped cream…

* * *

She moved restlessly in bed that night, finding sleep hard to come by and unable to get the *Whipped Cream* record sleeve out of her mind's eye.

I would never allow myself to be smothered in cream for any man's delectation, she reminded herself sternly, so why does it take me right back to Tom Hocking's bed? Why does it make me think of being naked in his arms and...*other delights*?

Why do I feel lonely and unfinished, edgy and aching with that special kind of longing?

Being in his bed and in his arms got to me, she acknowledged after some painful thought. Or he got to me, or a part of me I thought was dead and buried after Rob...

Strange, because he also scared me, and at most other times he annoys the life out of me. Then there's the long line of peachy blondes his own sister accused him of.

He's just too damned attractive, too... She stopped and sighed. And she recalled with sudden clarity the speculation she'd seen in three pairs of eyes, speculation to do with how she and Tom might have met in bed, even by mistake, and she shivered. Too attractive, and too clever, and now I think I even hate him, she reflected.

Tom Hocking didn't go to bed until midnight.

He got up from a table strewn with papers, stretched, and crossed the lounge of his hotel suite to the balcony where he stared over the beach and the sea. There was no moon but in the starlight a line of white surf was breaking on the beach. He could hear its rhythm and smell the salt in the air.

Strangely, since he hadn't thought of her for the hours since they'd parted, he discovered Chas Bartlett was on his mind.

Something of a surprise, he conceded. He could have sworn she hadn't been physically unmoved by their encounter in his bed. He'd even tended to take her explanation of how she'd got there with a pinch of salt. Heaven alone knew, he'd come across some extremely ingenious women in his time including one who had done exactly that—smuggled herself into his bed—but now he had to wonder. She was exhibiting all the signs of being an iron maiden. A smile touched his lips as the thought crossed his mind.

Unfortunately—the smile became dry—he'd discovered that he was more moved by that encounter than he'd expected. Or at least, he corrected himself, the mental image of her glorious hair, her smooth, slim body, those tantalising legs in that damned slip of a nightgown had taken to popping into his mind when he least expected it.

But would it lead him to do any more about it? Laying siege to an iron maiden wasn't exactly his style. There was Vanessa's wedding to get to the altar. There was the fact that he was contemplating changing his lifestyle rather drastically.

Room for an unusual but prickly girl who intrigued him none the less? No, he decided. So he'd have to hope those inconvenient images of her in his bed—he grimaced—went away. Or replace them with a flesh and blood girl who didn't object to being in his bed…

It was a stroke of fate that provided one unique touch for the Weaver-Hocking wedding.

Chas went to a concert at Queensland University, her

Alma Mater, and one of the acts impressed her tremendously. It was a troupe of jugglers, four of them, dressed in white catsuits spangled with gold and silver, with white face paint and, for the girls, pink cherry-blossom headdresses.

Not only did they juggle balls and hoops, but they also danced to the lovely background music in what was an ethereal, delicate display of rhythm and movement. Not a word was spoken, hand gestures said it all.

Chas sat entranced and, at the end of the twenty-minute routine, decided she had to have this act for Vanessa's wedding. It would be just perfect for during the meal; it would supply the unique, memorable touch she was seeking.

It proved, she discovered when she went to visit the troupe backstage, to be havable. They travelled with their own props, their own music, and could weave their magic on a much smaller, portable stage than the University Great Hall's stage.

She went back to Cresswell Lodge several times over the next weeks but only for day trips, and she never once ran into Tom. She also kept in touch with Vanessa frequently by phone—persistence was the key to that, she discovered—and she really felt she had everything under control, including the touches that were going to make the Hocking-Weaver wedding uniquely memorable.

Then, about three weeks before the wedding, two things happened in quick succession.

A friend she hadn't seen since their university days came back into her life; and she got an ultimatum from Tom Hocking.

*   *   *

Holly Maguire was the same age as Chas and they'd done their Bachelor of Arts together. But, whereas Chas had gone into wedding design, Holly had taken her bubbly personality, her lovely gold hair and curvy figure to Warwick, the country town on the Darling Downs, to teach art history at a private school.

It was a different Holly who met Chas for dinner and a reunion. She was still lovely but her natural bubbliness seemed now to be forced. They exchanged their news over a four-year gap while they ate pasta and drank red wine.

At one stage Holly said, 'Chas, someone told me you were getting married? It was a few years back but I didn't hear any more.'

'I was but we called it off,' Chas replied, as she'd replied more times than she cared to remember.

'What a pity you didn't get to design your own wedding!'

'Oh, I did,' Chas said unguardedly and grimaced. 'I—we only called it off about a week before the event. Mind you,' she hastened to add, 'it wasn't a large wedding; just family.'

Holly looked taken aback. 'Why so late?'

Chas lifted her shoulders. 'Irreconcilable differences. But tell me about your love life. I'm sure it's been much more exciting than mine.'

Holly stared at her then turned away with a hand to her mouth and tears in her eyes.

'What?' Chas asked softly.

The other girl sighed. 'I got ditched and the problem is, although it happened a few months ago, I can't forget him, I can't forgive him, I can't—seem to move on. That's why I made myself come away in the end, but I've got the horrible feeling I left my heart behind.'

'So he was special but like the devil all rolled into one?' Chas suggested.

'How well you put it.' Holly was weeping openly now. 'One of the things I hated myself for was, well, so many women fall under his spell and I hated being one of a crowd.'

Chas's eyes widened. 'Not all at the same time?'

'Oh, no. We had an affair, I got to meet the family and all the rest of it.' Holly gestured. 'I got really friendly with Vanessa—she's his sister—and I thought it would lead to marriage with all the trimmings but it didn't.'

'Warwick,' Chas mused and her eyes almost crossed. 'That's not far from Gladfield, right?'

'Right. They have a stud—'

But Chas broke in, 'A sister called Vanessa!' She sat back. 'Don't tell me we're talking about Tom Hocking?'

'Yes. Do you know him?'

'I do. I knew it!' she said triumphantly.

Holly looked bewildered. 'What?'

'That he's a womaniser *par excellence*! Holly,' Chas paused and put her hand over the other girl's, 'I'm so sorry. Here.' She handed the other girl her hanky.

For some reason, Chas lay in bed that night thinking about her ex-fiancé. Had he been special and like the devil all rolled into one, as she'd intimated to Holly? A good-looking man who'd got away with murder, as she'd intimated to Vanessa Hocking? Or just a man with a past?

He'd certainly been good-looking, he'd certainly been charismatic, sexy and irresistible to her. Until, to her everlasting mortification, her growing doubts about the depth of his commitment to her had crystallised a week before the wedding and she'd confronted him about it.

He'd admitted painfully that there'd been another woman in his life, a woman he couldn't have, a woman he was sure he'd put behind him. He'd said he was quite sure that once they were married, all memories of her would fade.

But that hadn't been good enough for Chas. Her slow descent from Cloud Nine had accelerated into an undignified tumble as she'd grappled with the realisation that she was in love with a man on the rebound. She'd called the wedding off and they'd parted, badly. He'd accused her of making a mountain out of a mole-hill—what was past was past and he'd have made sure it stayed that way. He'd insisted they would have been good together.

She'd told him 'good together' wasn't enough for her; told him he hadn't been honest with her.

His parting shot had been, 'Does any of this make a difference to the fact that you fell head over heels in love with me?'

To this day, she mused after her meeting with Holly Maguire, it was a conundrum that still plagued her. Had she really fallen head over heels in love with Rob Whitelaw? Or had she mistaken merely an attraction to a dynamic man for love? Compounded by the fact that she'd never fallen in love before, and made more confusing by a certain deficiency in her she'd told no one about…

Two days later she responded to a phone call. Tom Hocking was on the other end of the line.

'Oh,' she said, 'it's you.'

'What's that supposed to mean?' he growled down the line.

'Nothing,' Chas replied neutrally. 'How's it going up there?'

'It's not, any more. Things have taken an unexpected turn—'

'But that can't be!' Chas broke in. 'Everything's in place, everything to do with my end of things. Vanessa adores the dress, all the dresses, and she's perfectly happy with all the arrangements in fact, so—'

'I'm telling you, Charity Bartlett,' he said ominously, 'we are in disarray and unless you get your delicious derrière up here, and you stay up and take over the reins, there will be no wedding and you will lose a nice fat commission.'

Chas gasped. 'How dare you?'

'Refer to your delicious derrière? OK, I'll rephrase— get your eminently attractive personage up here. The rest stands.'

Chas swallowed some of her ire with difficulty. 'But what's gone so wrong?'

'The groom's parents have arrived. It turns out they're quite bitter about Rupert's decision to get married in Australia rather than upholding the centuries-old tradition of Wickham sons and heirs doing it in the ancestral hall.'

'It is the bride's prerogative,' Chas ventured.

'Perhaps, but it's thrown my mother thoroughly on her mettle. For example, not content with two horses and one carriage, she's got three carriages and six horses now. She's also drummed up a posse of look-alike fox-hunters to accompany the bridal coach. Oh, and the bride, incidentally, is suffering from extreme nerves and wondering if she's doing the right thing.'

'I…' Chas paused and controlled a wild impulse to laugh. 'There's nothing I can do about that—any of that!'

'Then you're fired,' Tom Hocking grated down the line.

'Hang on—you can't just fire me!'

'Oh, yes, I can. Not only can but will.'

'Listen to me, Mr Hocking—'

'No, you listen to me, Chas. If you can't organise a wedding that at least gets to the altar, you're misrepresenting yourself if nothing else. So either you get yourself up here pronto or the deal's off and I get someone else.'

He put the phone down hard.

Chas swore—with feeling.

CHAPTER FOUR

IN CONTRAST to her first visit to Cresswell Lodge, only Tom was home when she arrived a day later, although Piccanin and Leroy greeted her like a long-lost friend.

Early spring had given way to summer and the gardens of Cresswell Lodge were glorious.

If only it doesn't rain on the day, Chas thought as she looked around and sniffed the rose-scented air, this will be a picture-book wedding.

Then she became aware of Tom leaning against a pillar on the veranda, watching her.

She licked her lips and found, for a long, strange moment, that she was rooted to the spot as their gazes clashed and an electric current seemed to crackle between them.

She blinked several times to break the contact, and wondered if she was going mad. She'd convinced herself there was nothing to admire about Tom Hocking, however rich and famous he might be, however attractive; that those crazy moments of feeling as if she'd all along been destined to end up in his bed were sheer insanity.

Admittedly, all that convincing hadn't been as easy as she'd expected. And, if she was honest, the mental girding of her loins she'd undertaken every time she'd driven up to Cresswell, along with the cool stratagems she'd devised for keeping him at bay, had resulted in her feeling slightly foolish when he'd never been home.

He straightened at last and strolled towards her. He

was in stud-master mode—jeans, a work shirt and boots. 'Long time no see, Miss Bartlett,' he drawled, 'but we still strike sparks, I gather.'

Chas opened her mouth to deny it but the look in his grey eyes told her she was wasting her time, and there was only one thing to do: ignore it.

She said instead, 'This had better be good! If you think it's easy for me to drop everything and come up here at a minute's notice for three *weeks*, you're mistaken.'

He reached into her car and pulled out her two bags. 'Wait and see,' he advised. 'Is this it?'

'Yes, for the time being. Where is everyone?' She looked around.

'Gone to the races. We have the place to ourselves for a few hours.'

Chas looked exasperated. '*We* don't need time together.'

'I disagree.' He paused and frowned. 'What's got into you?'

'I—I don't know what you mean. You must admit you were extremely abusive on the phone!'

He put her bags on the ground and stuck his hands on his hips. 'And *you* appeared to have gone from regarding me as some form of low life, to some *lower* form of life,' he shot back.

Chas hesitated. 'This is very disruptive for me—can't you see that?'

'You didn't know that when you first spoke to me on the phone,' he pointed out. 'When you said,' he elucidated, '"Oh, it's you"—as if I were Dracula himself.'

'All right, that's more or less what I do think of you,'

she shot back. 'One of my friends is an emotional wreck, thanks to you!'

He blinked. 'Which one?'

Chas suffered a pang of remorse. She'd never intended to get into this with him; apart from anything else, it was like breaking a trust placed in her. Why didn't she stop and think rather than rushing in where angels feared to tread?

It struck her almost immediately that she usually did; that this kind of behaviour was quite out of character for her. So what did it mean?

For some reason, this man got to her and altered her reactions even when she'd sworn that, from a career point of view if nothing else, she would not cross swords with him again.

She turned away. 'It doesn't matter.' She reached for her handbag and closed the car door. 'Lead on, Mr Hocking,' she added drily.

'So I'm not to be allowed to defend myself?' he queried, not budging an inch.

Chas gestured. 'I shouldn't have brought it up. I'm sorry.'

'Let's see—would it be Holly Maguire?'

Chas froze and her wide, horrified gaze gave her away completely. 'How…how did you know?' she stammered.

'You obviously imagine I have a whole cast of emotionally wrecked women to choose from,' he said with satanic irony. 'I don't.'

'You mean you usually love 'em and leave 'em glowing with happiness?' she fired back. 'All these peachy blondes? That technique must have deserted you with Holly.'

'There's only one way to find out how…effective

my techniques are, Ms Bartlett. Care to road-test 'em? We are alone.' He looked around then looked into her eyes with a sardonic challenge in his own.

Chas was lost for words. She was also pink with embarrassment and quivering finely down the length of her body, as she had no doubt he was mentally undressing her.

'Perhaps we should just leave it there,' she managed to say stiffly.

'Oh, definitely,' he agreed, 'if you're referring to what was between Holly and myself. It was no one's business but our own. But there are generally two sides to a story, Chas Bartlett, and it might be a good idea if you reminded yourself of that.'

Annoyance at being lectured like this started to seep through her veins but she decided to hide it, and to change the subject completely. 'Tell me about the bridegroom's p—'

She stopped as a tall boy, about fifteen, tore around the corner of the house, obviously in distress.

'Tom,' he gasped, 'come quickly! Adam's driven the ute into the old shed wall and it's fallen down on top of him—I can't get him out and Mum's gone to town.'

'Bloody hell,' Tom snapped. 'That kid will give me grey hairs.' He hesitated briefly. 'Can we use your Rover, Chas? It'll save a few minutes.'

'Of course.' She dug into her jeans pocket and handed him the keys. 'I'll come too, I may be able to help.'

'By way of introduction,' Tom said to Chas, as he gunned the Range Rover down the drive, 'this is Brendan Baxter—' he gestured to the lad in the back seat '—and Adam is his younger brother. Quite the naughtiest and most accident-prone child I've ever met.'

'You're not wrong,' Brendan supplied with strong emotion. 'I was supposed to be keeping an eye on him but it's like…' He stopped helplessly and shook his head. 'Mum will murder me and everyone else has gone to the races!'

'Stay calm, kid,' Tom advised. 'He does have more lives than a cat.'

The old shed, timber and hung with a yellow allamanda creeper in full bloom, must have been picturesque before ten-year-old Adam Baxter had driven a ute through it. Now it looked like a collapsed bundle of weathered planks, although part of the roof was still up, and only the tailgate of the ute was visible.

Tom swore even more ferociously as he slammed the Range Rover to a stop.

'Maybe we need the fire department and an ambulance,' Chas suggested anxiously.

'We do but it could take them an hour to get here so I'll do a quick recce.' Tom got out. 'Brendan, go and ring 000 and tell them what's happened.'

'I've got my mobile,' Chas offered. She got it out of her bag and handed it to him.

Ten minutes later, in a display of strength that Chas secretly found awesome, Tom, with help from her and Brendan, had burrowed through the mess of timber so they had a view through the open passenger window into the ute. The driver's side was completely blocked.

Dark-haired and pale-faced with a bleeding cut on his forehead, Adam Baxter was slumped down into the far corner of the driver's seat. His head would barely have risen above the steering wheel, but, although barely perceptibly, he was breathing. He was also buckled into a seat belt.

'At least he did that,' Tom said grimly. 'It might have saved him from going through the windscreen but it could also make it harder to get him out.' He tried the handle but the door was jammed. He leant in as far as he could but couldn't reach the boy.

'If he's unconscious, we shouldn't move him in case of head or neck injury,' said Chas. 'At least, I think—'

They all froze at an ominous crack overhead.

'There's no choice,' Tom said coolly but rapidly. 'We need to get him out as quickly as possible before the rest of it comes crashing down. I'm going to try and get in through the window. You and Brendan go back the way we came in, fast!'

'Hang on.' Chas swallowed. 'I'm the slimmest of the three of us; I'll get in more easily. Perhaps you and Brendan can bolster the roof up while I do?'

Tom Hocking hesitated and Chas took her chance— she wriggled her way through the window head first. It was a tight squeeze and there wasn't much room to manoeuvre once she was in but she managed to release the seat belt. She moved backwards, pulling the unconscious boy carefully with her at the same time. Once she was up against the door, she turned round with great difficulty.

'Help me out,' she panted. 'At least you can reach him now.'

They manhandled her out and set her on her feet. 'Watch that beam,' Tom ordered and Chas saw that he'd propped a sturdy beam up to act as a bolster to the roof.

'Here we go.' And he, as gently as possible, lifted

the unconscious child out through the window. 'Let's get out of here!'

They'd barely got out when the rest of the roof crashed down onto the ute.

Tom laid Adam down on the ground on his side. 'That was a close call.'

Chas put her hand to her face as her legs buckled and she sank to the ground next to the prostrate boy. Brendan simply stared at the remains of the shed with his mouth hanging open.

Tom knelt down beside Adam and felt for a pulse. 'OK, troops,' he said quietly, 'don't ever disobey my orders again—except when they need to be disobeyed. You're two brave customers!'

Chas had lifted her head incredulously at the first part of his statement, but what she encountered, as their gazes clashed, was genuine admiration in his grey eyes.

'Thanks,' she murmured. 'How is he?'

Tom turned back to Adam. 'I think he's just knocked himself out.'

Brendan knelt in the dirt beside his brother. Then he jumped up as a siren became audible. Several minutes later, the ambulance arrived with a fire engine in hot pursuit.

'Well,' Tom said, as he and Chas watched the ambulance and fire engine depart, 'what we need is a drink.'

The consensus of opinion had been that Adam Baxter was not gravely injured in any way but would need treatment for concussion as well as a couple of stitches in his forehead. Brendan had gone in the ambulance with his brother. Tom had contacted the boys' mother and arranged for her to meet them at the local hospital.

He'd also recommended to Mary Baxter that she not be too hard on either boy, although he would certainly have a word with Adam when he was better.

'Don't they have a father?' Chas queried as they were driving back to the homestead.

'No. Part of the problem.' Tom grimaced. 'He ran off with another woman several years ago.'

'So they—do they live here?'

'Yep. Mary's worked on the stud for years. She's a genius at schooling weanlings, young horses, breaking them in to lead, accept a bridle and so on. She's far more successful with horses than with her own boys, which is why I find myself standing *in loco parentis* at times. But they're not bad kids, really. And Brendan is developing a nice way with horses himself. I've given him a part-time job.'

He slowed down as they breasted the rise and cruised down towards the house. 'Uh-oh!'

'What?' Chas enquired, then she saw for herself.

Both her nylon bags, left standing on the driveway in the emergency, had been torn open, and Leroy and Piccanin were romping around the lawn having a field-day with their contents. Her clothes, her underwear, her cosmetics were strewn everywhere, and Leroy had somehow got his head through the leg hole of a very delicate pair of peach silk knickers.

Her mouth fell open until she clicked it shut quite painfully. 'I don't believe it,' she whispered.

Tom turned to her and slid his arm along the back of her seat. 'My abject apologies, but…' he paused and searched her eyes '…it does have a—funny side?'

Chas hesitated for a split-second then she started to gurgle with laughter.

And when Tom, grinning, pulled her into his arms, they laughed together, and even harder.

'Thank heavens I didn't leave my purse or my brief-case on the drive!' Chas gasped. 'Do they do this often?'

'It's a first so far as I know,' Tom returned, 'but Leroy's little more than a puppy.'

'Holy smoke! How much more has he got to grow? And why Leroy?'

'We named him after Leroy Loggins, one of those very tall basketball players. But not much more to grow, thank heavens.' Tom hugged her and then kissed her lightly. 'Let's see what we can retrieve, then we definitely deserve that drink!' He got out and whistled for the dogs. 'Leroy, you idiot, come here. If you could only see how stupid you look!'

Chas sat quite still for a moment as he disentangled Leroy from her knickers. Then she put two fingers lightly to her lips before she got out to help.

When they'd gathered everything up and deposited it on the veranda table, Tom disappeared inside.

He came back minutes later with a bottle of champagne in a silver bucket and two glasses.

'How lovely,' Chas said with feeling, as she went on sorting through her clothes. She'd established three piles, one for the irretrievable, one for stuff that needed to be laundered and one for stuff that had miraculously escaped all injury.

Tom popped the cork, poured and handed her a glass. She sipped and sank down into a chair with a sigh of pleasure. 'Thanks.'

'I'll replace it all for you,' he said, running his eye over the colourful piles. 'You could drive into Warwick or Toowoomba tomorrow. I don't know whether you'll find the haute cuisine—'

'That's food,' she broke in.

'The haute cuisine of fashion, I was about to say.' He grinned. 'But at least you could get enough to keep you going.'

'I might be able to keep going anyway. Some of it's OK. Thank heavens no one else was around to see Leroy wearing my undies on his head!'

'I'm only surprised they weren't,' he replied with a sudden touch of moodiness. 'It would have been par for the course for the kind of mayhem that's been going on lately.'

'Tell me about it,' Chas invited.

He looked heavenwards. 'Where to start? The funny thing is, individually, they're not too bad.' He shrugged. 'The Earl of Wickham is a bit overpowering. The Countess, well, she lives on another planet but then so does Clare. My mother…' He paused.

'You don't have to tell me.'

Tom sighed. 'Yes, I do. She's taken it as a personal insult, this business of them making plaintive remarks about what a break with tradition this wedding is. They're just not getting on!' he added with extreme frustration. 'Then there's Arnold.'

Chas, on her visits to Cresswell Lodge, had got to know Arnold, the tense young man who ran the household, a little better. She'd also formed the opinion that Arnold didn't really want to be known too well.

She looked blank. 'Arnold?'

'He's also taken it as a personal insult and he's liable to deliver their dinners into their laps one day.'

'Good heavens! Why?'

'Arnold is devoted to my mother since she rescued

him from an uncertain fate. He's the grandson of a former head stud groom, and Mother was the one who insisted that his erratic behaviour could be due to a mental condition. She was right. He was diagnosed as schizophrenic and she took him under her wing, she fostered his love of cooking, and he's been with us ever since.'

'Oh, dear,' Chas said gravely.

'Precisely. As for Vanessa, she's going out of her way to be extremely disruptive and, as I've known her since she was a baby—' he grimaced '—I can tell it's because she's not sure of herself over something.'

'To be honest, I've wondered about Rupert and Vanessa.'

'So have I.' Tom studied his glass. 'For all that we can clash, I'm very fond of Vanessa and if she has serious doubts, well…' He gestured and sighed. 'I get the feeling the reality of being whisked overseas to a new home, a new lifestyle, for all that it may be a pretty privileged one, is just hitting home. Vanessa really loves Cresswell.'

'Yes, she told me that. It may only be last-minute nerves, though. Some brides get them. So do some husbands-to-be,' Chas added drily. 'Are they staying here, the Wickhams?'

'Yes. Why?'

'It sounds to me as if we need to separate them selectively as much as possible before the wedding.'

'But his parents want to be with Rupert and they want to get to know Vanessa, so—'

'But me no buts,' Chas said with a tinge of humour. 'Don't you own a charter airline?'

He frowned then nodded.

'Have they ever been to Australia before?'

'No.'

'Then there's a whole wonderful country out there to show them! They could spend a few days on the Barrier Reef, a few more days at Ayers Rock, maybe a bit of time up at Kakadu. Rupert could go with them, maybe Vanessa as well.'

Chas paused. 'She might even find that, without the strain of having to be loyal to her mum, things improve. If nothing else, it will give them something else to think about and it may calm Vanessa's nerves. If you like, though, I could try to establish if she is having serious reservations. Sometimes it's easier to confide in an outsider.'

Tom Hocking drew a long, slow breath. 'Charity Bartlett, you've just cost me a small mint of money but you're a genius—why didn't I think of that?'

'I won't answer that,' she murmured with a glint of mischief.

He sat back. 'I—'

'There's only one problem with it,' Chas interrupted. 'Will your mother mind if Vanessa goes off for a bit with her prospective in-laws?'

He frowned. 'It's not as if she's going to lose Vanessa immediately. She and Rupert plan to be here for a while, at least. But—could you involve her a bit more in all the preparations?'

'I could,' Chas said slowly as she was struck by a sudden thought. 'Although…' She paused then continued on another tack, 'You were going to say? Before I interrupted.'

He looked at her thoughtfully. 'For two people who started out in a lot of discord today, we seem to have made some positive progress.'

Chas's eyes widened. She couldn't deny it. She'd

rescued a child with him, she'd laughed with and been hugged and kissed by him, she'd been impressed not only by his strength but also by other things about him that had emerged. His care and concern for Mary Baxter and her fatherless sons, for example.

Just to be sitting sipping champagne with him was pleasurable but...

She looked away suddenly as the warning bells that had rung in her mind a couple of minutes earlier rang again, and her expression closed.

'And what were you about to say before you changed your mind?' he queried, on a different note.

Chas hesitated.

'That you'd sorted things out so satisfactorily you could go back to Brisbane—if it wasn't for my mother?' he hazarded.

She looked back at him, trying to assess his change of mood. 'Would that be so—what would be so wrong about that?'

'Nothing. Unless you're regretting the positive progress we've made, Chas?'

She couldn't tear her gaze away from his, she found.

'Let's not beat about the bush,' he added. 'I'm still plagued by visions of you in a red silk nightie—and nothing else.'

Chas swallowed and rushed into speech without much thought. 'You didn't do anything about it.'

He smiled briefly. 'You made it perfectly plain you didn't want me to. Are you saying you're regretting that now?'

'No! I mean—I'm saying, if it meant anything to you, seriously, well...' She tailed off and took hold somewhat grimly as she castigated herself for once again letting this man trap her into unwary statements.

'Maybe seriousness doesn't come into it, if you see what I mean?'

'A fling with you, a tumble in the hay—you're suggesting that's all I'm after?' He raised his eyebrows. 'How the hell would you know what I have in mind?'

Chas cleared her throat. 'Perhaps the pertinent point is that I, for reasons best known to myself, am not willing to gamble on any man at the moment.'

'How so?'

'Uh—that's my business.'

'You mean you're lumping all men with the one who left you at the altar?' He stared at her. 'Think that's wise, or rational?'

'I think,' Chas said through her teeth, 'it's very wise. And it so happens *I* left *him* at the altar. Well, I called it off.' She stopped abruptly and frowned ferociously. 'Who told you that?'

He shrugged. 'Vanessa.'

'She just—came out and told you?'

He eyed her ironically. 'No, she didn't just come and tell me. I asked her what she knew about you.'

'Why?'

'Blame your red nightgown again.' He shrugged. 'Or your inability to tell your left from your right.'

'You didn't tell her *why* you were asking, did you?' Her gaze was horrified.

He permitted himself a faint smile. 'I told her you seemed to be unusually dedicated to your career. She replied that being left at the altar by some dashing, good-looking cad would no doubt account for it.'

Chas could have shot herself for confiding in Tom's sister.

'Incidentally,' he added, 'she also said that you were not into serious relationships any more.'

'I… I'm not. I, well—I'm not.'

'Could it be a case of the pot calling the kettle black, Chas, what you've accused me of, then?'

She bit her lip.

'Assuming it's not all men you're repelling,' he said, 'we might find we're better suited than you think if you're after no-strings-attached affairs.'

'It's not all men,' she replied sweetly although she was angry beneath it. 'Now, if Rupert Leeton, Lord Weaver, wasn't spoken for, for example, I wouldn't have minded getting to know him better.'

Tom's jaw dropped then he started to laugh.

'What I mean to say is that I rather prefer his kind of man,' Chas soldiered on. 'However…' she stood up and swept all her belongings into her arms, or attempted to '…that's my business, not yours. Am I in the same bedroom?'

'I have no idea. Perhaps a better idea,' he said as he stood up, 'would be to put you right next door to the bathroom.' He bent to retrieve a lacy black bra, an elegant tub of moisturiser and her cranberry silk nightgown. 'I'll bring these,' he added helpfully.

Chas made a strangled little sound. 'Who is likely to know which bedroom I've been allocated?'

He smiled quite ravishingly at her. 'Now I come to think of it, Arnold generally sticks a list up on the corkboard in the kitchen. We could consult that.'

'You're enjoying every minute of this, aren't you?' she accused him.

He looked down at his handful of her things. 'It certainly,' he said with suspicious gravity, 'brings back memories of being very up close and personal with you, Chas.'

She swung on her heel and marched inside towards the kitchen.

There was a list on the corkboard.

There was also a note to the effect that dinner would be served at seven o'clock sharp. Chas groaned as she read it.

Tom raised an eyebrow at her.

'The last dinner I had here was just—huge,' she said helplessly. 'And now I'll be more than ever afraid of offending the chef and ending up with some of it in my lap if I don't finish it,' she added darkly.

Tom grinned. 'Deference to my mother is the key. Just remember that. OK, it says here that Ms Bartlett has the cream bedroom in the west wing—you'll be relieved to know that this room does have its own bathroom. We've only just finished renovating it.'

Chas didn't deign to reply.

The cream bedroom was smaller than the last one she'd been allotted but it had a pretty view over the creek and it opened onto a side veranda.

She dumped all her belongings on the bed and turned to face Tom Hocking.

He handed her her nightgown and bra, and put the tub of moisturiser on the dressing table. 'I gather I'm about to get my marching orders.'

A little glint lit Chas's blue eyes. 'There is nothing more for you to do here,' she said evenly, then the glint became a flash of irritation. 'So stop trying to make me feel bad in some way!'

'Are you always this tetchy?'

'I'm not—I'm…' She trailed off and shrugged.

He folded his arms across his chest. 'In lots of ways

you are like a battering ram in a velvet glove,' he reflected.

Chas blinked. 'A *what*?'

He smiled fleetingly. 'I decided that whoever took on this job would need to be just that,' he explained. 'And apart from the unexpected complication of Rupert's parents, you did impose much more order than I thought possible. It's therefore rather ironic that I should object to finding myself on the receiving end of your powerful personality beneath that deceptive exterior.'

Chas opened her mouth to deny the charge but changed her mind several times.

Finally, she said quietly, 'It's only logic, practicality and, I guess, a feel for things that's seen me succeed with weddings.' She paused, studied her hands then looked into his eyes. 'If you feel you've run into a brick wall on a personal level, I'm sorry, but I can't help it.'

He said nothing for a long moment but as they gazed at each other, Chas began to wonder how right she was in her statement that she 'couldn't help it'.

There was no amusement in his grey gaze. It was entirely level and completely absorbed in her—and it did strange things to her.

It opened what had been a closed door for the last couple of years, onto an area of her soul that had been cauterised, or so she'd thought. It wasn't a physical area, it was the emotional need for a man that suddenly hit her beneath Tom Hocking's searching gaze.

It was the company, the friendship, the laughter, the differences that could be so complementary, as exemplified by their time together this afternoon before their current debate had started to rage.

Was she ready for that again after the barren years, she wondered, if not the whole experience? Could you have one without the other? Would that come too and not in a despised way because of her memories?

She trembled and he saw it—and all of a sudden that charge was there between them again. She was conscious of the way his hair fell, the set of his shoulders beneath a now dirty shirt. She was aware of his hard, flat diaphragm and lean hips in dusty jeans.

All his endeavours to free young Adam Baxter had left a faint odour of sweat on his clothes that was intensely masculine.

And she remembered suddenly that his were the only hands that had caressed her body in a long time, and they'd done so briefly but with knowledge, experience and sheer artistry.

A dew of sweat broke out on her brow and she moved restlessly as all sorts of sensations raced across her skin.

He spoke at last. 'But did I run into a brick wall? I don't happen to think so. There were moments of mutual interest, Charity Bartlett. You can deny them until you're blue in the face but I won't ever believe you.'

'You...you scared the living daylights out of me,' she objected.

'I meant to scare the living daylights out of you,' he said with a tinge of impatience. 'I'm a little tired of finding strange women in my bed.'

Her eyes widened. 'How often does it happen?'

'It has happened before,' he stated grimly. 'But I only share my bed on invitation.'

'Yet you were prepared to make an exception for me!' she suggested scathingly.

He smiled. 'No. I was prepared to frighten you a bit

for your own good and prove to you—whoever you were—that I prefer to choose my bedmates. As it turned out, we both got a bit of a surprise.'

Chas swallowed.

'Yes,' he said, and stepped forward to close the gap between them. 'Your skin was like satin, your body was gorgeous—I've told you about your legs.' He smiled absently. 'And for a moment, suspended in time, our bodies spoke to each other in rather an explicit way, don't you agree? I could see it in your eyes. I could feel it beneath my hands.'

He put his hands on her shoulders and looked down into her eyes. 'Tell me it's changed, Chas.'

She couldn't. The feel of his hands cupping her shoulders seemed to burn through the stuff of her blouse and that *frisson* he'd brought her in his bed flowered through her body again in all her secret places.

She closed her eyes and gritted her teeth. It would be the easiest thing in the world to succumb to the pure pleasure of his arms, that beautiful, masculine body and the way their bodies did speak to each other.

It would be only natural to draw his hands down to cover her breasts, to slide her hands beneath his shirt, to explore him intimately…

She held her breath as he moved and did just what her body was begging for—he moved his hands down to her breasts and a ripple of pure sensuality flowed downwards to her very core.

Nor could she hide what was happening to her. She couldn't tear her gaze from his, she couldn't conceal the little gasp of pleasure that rose to her lips or the way her eyes widened in wonder.

'See what I mean?' he murmured. 'And in case you have any doubts, it's mutual.'

She bit her lip, and was only saved from herself by a memory that floated into her mind, of her wedding dress taunting her as it hung on the rail in her wardrobe unworn on what was to have been her wedding day.

'I…' she said with utter concentration. 'I'm sorry but I can't do it. Please don't bring this up between us again.'

He took his hands away and shoved them into his pockets. 'If that ever changes, let me know.'

He walked away and closed the door behind him.

Chas hugged herself, closed her eyes and stood deep in incredulous thought. The words that drifted through her brain were: *Here I go again.*

'No,' she whispered. 'No, no way.'

CHAPTER FIVE

FOR the next few days the families, both Weaver and Hocking, closed over her like a wave, engulfing her in their turmoil but at the same time protecting her from Tom Hocking and his dangerous effect on her. Or almost.

Not that it closed down her thoughts on the matter entirely, and she did run into him twice, once verbally, once physically.

She was a jogger. She'd been good at athletics at school, especially running, and the habit had become ingrained. At Cresswell, she got into the habit of jogging for half an hour before breakfast or after dinner. Both Leroy and Piccanin, great fans of this habit of hers, were with her when she ran down the drive back towards the house one early morning as the sun was rising.

Tom was just leaving the house as she arrived on the lawn.

'Ah, the flying filly,' he drawled.

Chas stopped in her tracks, breathing heavily. 'You may think it's complimentary to compare me to a horse but I don't,' she panted.

He studied her comprehensively, all the sweat-licked length of her beneath a singlet and running shorts. 'Well, I do admire horses,' he said with a shrug, 'and perhaps you should blame that gorgeous mane of hair and those long legs?' He strolled on his way.

She put her hands to her hair and glanced down her

body. How dared he make her so aware of herself even when he was comparing her to a horse? How dared he bring to mind the two of them together—? No, stop, Chas, she commanded herself. Go and have a cold shower rather than even thinking about Tom Hocking in that way...

The next time she ran into him she was perfectly groomed, in jeans and a black T-shirt, with her hair plaited in a severe Indian braid. Unfortunately, she also literally ran into him.

It was a wet day. She'd leapt out of her Ranger Rover and sprinted for the house with a clutch of parcels and no hand free for her umbrella.

She cannoned into him as he was about to step off the veranda, and she dropped everything.

'Still flying,' he observed, circling her waist with his hands in a lightning reflex to stop her from being bowled over.

'It's raining!' she pointed out raggedly as she caught her breath.

'People usually protect themselves from the rain. Look at me.'

She did. He wore a caped oilskin coat and a broad-brimmed felt hat.

'Very bushranger,' she said. 'I do own an umbrella; I just didn't have a free hand.'

'That explains it.' But he, rather pointedly, didn't release her.

They stared into each other's eyes for a long moment. Chas was supremely conscious of his hands on her waist and how the feel of them was causing her colour to fluctuate. She was also unable to tear her gaze from the planes and angles of his face, those riveting smoky eyes and the expression in them that told her he was very much aware of her delicious unease.

Delicious unease? she wondered, and swallowed. What a contradiction in terms—but didn't that just about sum up her whole stance on the subject of Tom Hocking?

'You know,' he said, as if he were a mind-reader, 'there are certain inconsistencies in your powerful personality, Ms Bartlett.'

She blinked then looked annoyed. 'It's not powerful!'

'It is,' he disagreed. 'You're very self-assured most of the time yet you blush like a virgin at other times. Right now, for example.'

Chas tore herself out of his grasp and bent down to retrieve her parcels.

'Are you a virgin?' He picked up a packet and handed it to her.

'No! I'm not. It's purely to do with how we met!'

'Not easy to forget, huh?'

Chas closed her eyes.

When she opened them, he murmured, 'Funny thing is, I have the same problem,' and walked away into the rain.

For the next couple of days she was often in his company, at meals and at the elegant soirée held to introduce some of the leading lights of the district to the Wickhams, although she was never alone with him.

She did discover that when he was present at a meal, for example, things ran smoothly; when he wasn't they could be a little jagged. And she was forced to ponder the invisible air of authority he exerted so that even Earl Wickham deferred to him.

It came to her that there was more power and cleverness behind Tom Hocking than she'd given him credit for, even when she'd realised the kind of circles he moved in.

But of course he couldn't be around all the time, and when he wasn't the difficulties lurking below the surface for the rest of the wedding party became obvious.

Individually, she quite liked the earl and countess— he was tall and rotund, she was tall and thin and reminded Chas of a rather vague crane—but there was no doubting their underlying air of *We'll just have to make the best of this!*

Then there was Harriet. Her prickly state of mind was obvious. And Vanessa was giving a good imitation of the flighty, expensive socialite she could do so well but wasn't underneath, as Chas had come to appreciate over the last few months. Clare and Rupert simply looked uncomfortable a lot of the time.

With sudden visions of this wedding slipping away from her, Chas swung into action.

She took pains with the Wickhams and managed to establish a rapport between Helen, Countess Wickham, and Clare over fine English porcelain. She discovered that the earl loved nothing so much as gardening. If there was one thing other than horses that Harriet was passionate about, it was her garden. With infinite tact, she drew them together on the subject.

Vanessa, however, proved to be a harder nut to crack, and that really worried Chas, until the night of the soirée.

She hadn't planned to attend the soirée.

She had relieved Harriet of her involvement in its last-minute preparations. She'd bearded Arnold in his kitchen, told him about her father's gourmet delicatessen and café, and offered her help. She'd also explained that above all she wanted to help Harriet in any way she could.

Arnold had accepted, and between them and another kitchen hand they'd produced a marvellous array of savouries and canapés, hot titbits and the punch to end all punches. As the center-piece of the main table Chas had arranged a basket of flowers from the garden that was quite stunning.

'There.' She stood back and eyed it. 'Not bad!'

'Brilliant!' Harriet came in looking rested, relaxed and almost regal in a sapphire-blue dress with pearls in her ears and around her throat. 'You are a darling, Chas! Arnold is so impressed and everything seems to be so much easier when you're around, I don't know why but it does—but you're not ready!'

'Oh, I wasn't coming to the party,' Chas explained. 'This is part of my commission as the wedding consultant.' She grinned fleetingly.

'Oh, yes, you are coming to the party!' Harriet insisted. 'I simply won't take no for an answer. Off you go.' She gave Chas a gentle push towards the door.

Fortunately the one dressy outfit Chas had brought had escaped Leroy and Piccanin's attentions. It was a silky wrap dress that clung to her slender figure and had a deep V-neckline and tiny cap sleeves. The silk was a pale dusky pink and patterned with tiny deeper pink and green flower sprays. With it she usually wore dangly earrings and backless green suede stilettos.

She paused in front of the mirror and held the dress in front of her. In view of Harriet's resplendence it would be just about right, she decided, but grimaced at her reflection. Her hair and her hands, after several hours of working in the kitchen, were ordinary, to put it mildly—well, she would a be bit late, that was all, while she attended to them.

Just under an hour later, she stared at herself in the long closet-door mirror. Her hair shone but was restrained at her neck. Her skin gleamed, more golden than pale with the advance of summer—but the dress?

She bit her lip. The *décolletage* was the problem, the rest of it was fine. Nor did it usually bother her—it wasn't that low, but it did expose the shadowed valley between her breasts rather more than might be—what?

Be wise with a man in the house who not infrequently studied her figure? A man who'd seen her virtually undressed, come to that.

She tugged at the neckline then rattled through the rest of her wardrobe. There was nothing else remotely suitable—why on earth hadn't she taken up Tom's offer to replenish her wardrobe? What say she didn't make an appearance? Would anyone miss her?

Harriet knocked on her door and called her name through the panels.

Chas gritted her teeth. 'Just coming,' she called back.

For some reason—wouldn't you know it?—the first gaze she encountered across a crowded room when she finally arrived at the party was Tom's. And time seemed to stand still as he looked her up and down, and raised his glass to her. Then people came between them and he turned away.

She didn't come into contact with him again until about an hour later, by which time she'd made an important discovery.

She'd gone out onto the veranda for some fresh air,

confident that the soirée was going well: that the Wickhams were in top form and not lamenting anything; that Harriet was in top form but not going over the top; and Clare was enjoying herself so much she was just a little tipsy.

She froze, though, and retreated into the shadows as she heard Vanessa saying from further down the veranda, 'I'm sorry, I'm sorry, I'm sorry!'

'Darling,' Rupert's voice, 'it's OK.'

'How can it be OK? I've been so bitchy lately and…and do you know what I'd like to do? Just run away with you to a registry office. I never could handle a lot of pomp and ceremony, it gives me the yips. Why did I ever go along with all this?'

'Vannie,' Rupert said steadily, 'so long as it's not *me*, I understand, sweetheart.'

'It's not you. It's my mother, it's your mother and father and what they're going to expect of me—why did you have to be the son of an earl, Rupe? And live so far away?'

'We'll live wherever you're happy, sweetheart. Because if you're not happy, I never will be. I love you, Vanessa Harriet Hocking. I always will.'

'Oh, Rupe, I love you too.'

The apparent contradictions in all this didn't escape Chas, but it did reassure her. If anyone should be suffering from pre-wedding nerves, highly strung Vanessa was an obvious candidate.

On the other hand, if anyone was going to get her through it, it was Rupert himself.

She stole back inside and bumped into Tom.

He took her empty glass, gestured to a waiter who normally worked as a stable hand and procured a fresh glass of wine for her.

'I believe I have to thank you for this evening's success, Chas. Not only that but also a distinct lessening of the overall tension.'

'I probably helped a little.' She shrugged. 'But I do have some good news for you.' And she recounted the conversation she'd just heard outside.

He took a startled breath, then said, 'That's the best news I've heard for a while.'

She smiled. 'Same here.'

Something in his eyes changed. 'You're looking,' he said slowly as his gaze ran down her dress and came back to rest on her *décolletage*, 'positively peachy, Ms Bartlett.'

Chas swallowed. He might as well have his fingers on her breasts from the reaction his gaze was having. As for his description of her, it caused her eyes to darken and caused her to say ominously, 'Peachy?'

'Ah. Bad choice of words, I gather. You know,' he added, 'if I'd had all the peachy blondes who have been attributed to me, I'd be dead from overwork. Also, you're a brunette. Aren't they supposed to be the ones men marry?'

Chas chose to answer this with the best *non sequitur* she could come up with. 'You're not looking too bad yourself, Mr Hocking. Very Savile Row.' His charcoal suit was beautifully tailored. 'Very—experienced and Don Juanish, even if you have been maligned to a certain extent.'

He inspected the little pulse beating rather rapidly at the base of her throat, and smiled absently just as a couple came up to them.

He turned to greet them and introduce them.

'Chas, meet Lorna and Carl Philips. Carl and Lorna, this is our marriage consultant extraordinaire, Charity

Bartlett.' He added, only for Chas's ears, 'Alias Aphrodite.'

'Oh, good,' Lorna Philips said enthusiastically. 'I did want to meet you! The thing is, our daughter is getting married soon…'

Chas forced her attention towards Lorna and tried to concentrate, although it was difficult with her pulses clamouring and, as the result of just two words, the memory of being in his bed suddenly centre stage in her mind's eye. Tom himself murmured that he'd leave them to it, and he walked away.

Alias Aphrodite, Chas thought as she stared out of her bedroom window. If only he knew just how far she fell short of a 'goddess of love' description.

The house was quiet now, the garden silvered by starlight. She guessed that everyone was in bed. She was ready for bed herself and had turned the light off.

Then she saw a shadow detach itself from the veranda. There was no one else in the house that tall, so it had to be Tom, and she saw Leroy and Piccanin race up to him, be patted and subside at his feet.

He stood out in the garden for nearly ten minutes, as if he was deep in thought.

What, she wondered, could he be thinking about?

It came to her abruptly that there were times when Tom Hocking retreated from the fray of his family; when he looked around with a withdrawn expression that seemed to say: I put up with all this because I have to but I'd rather be a million miles away.

She shivered suddenly, although it wasn't cold. Because he was a hard man to read and understand? Because she was suddenly possessed of an overwhelming desire to go out to him and try to break through the barriers she sensed around him?

What does it have to do with you, though? she asked herself. We decided we weren't going down that road, didn't we?

She went to Toowoomba the next day and enlisted the help of Birdie Tait. She'd already met Birdie a couple of times, and together they drew up itineraries, made reservations and sought selectively to separate the wedding party for its own good.

'This is inspired,' Birdie said to Chas a day later. 'I see why Laura Richmond recommended you so highly, although I had my doubts…' Birdie broke off a little awkwardly.

'Because I'm a woman? Birdie!' Chas remonstrated. They'd become goods friends in a short space of time. 'I bet without you the Hocking empire would fall apart at the seams.'

Birdie went pink with pleasure although she denied the charge. 'It wasn't that, anyway,' she added. 'It's just that Tom can be…well, falling in love with him has become something of a local pastime, and not only local.'

'Ah.' Chas continued sorting accommodation vouchers. 'I got the feeling that might be the case.'

'I would love to see him married and with children,' Birdie said with real longing. 'I'm sure he'd make a marvellous husband and father.'

'What makes you so sure?' Chas looked up with a frown.

'He's a lot like his father. I have no doubt Andrew sowed a few wild oats—although you have no idea what lengths some women will go to to bring themselves to Tom's attention! But once his father settled down with Harriet it was…' Birdie gestured with a curious touch of sadness '…it was a love match for the thirty-odd years they were together.'

'Has he ever shown any inclination to settle down?'

'Only once. There was someone, Sarah Oldfield, her name was, but that's a few years ago. They seemed to be really close and I guess we all thought… But, in the end, she married someone else.' Here, Birdie permitted herself a small smile. 'I sometimes think he needs a saint, but would that be what he wants?'

Chas stared at her for a moment with her lips parted. Despite her almost adoration of Tom Hocking, had Birdie put her finger on the kind of man he was?

But what kind of a man was he really? Could one believe in the long line of peachy blondes or was that the barbed kind of remark Vanessa might make when she was annoyed with him? Holly had also mentioned a long line, but were Birdie and Tom himself more accurate in their assessments? Did women throw themselves at him? It was possible, she had to concede.

Then again, poor Holly, even if there were two sides to a story, didn't rate a mention!

CHAPTER SIX

CHAS came back from Toowoomba ten days after she'd arrived at Cresswell to find two large parcels on her bed.

She opened them, studied the contents with a frown, then decided she had to seek out the master of Cresswell Lodge in relation to those contents.

He was in his study, working at his desk.

'Ah, the wedding consultant,' he murmured, and eyed her as she placed two bags on the desk. 'You don't have to thank me for those, it was the least I could do. But sit down. I wanted to talk to you anyway.'

Chas remained standing. Once again, Tom was formally attired in a white shirt with a navy pinstripe, a silvery tie and lightweight grey suit, the jacket of which hung over the back of his chair.

It reinforced that impressive dimension to him, she decided. You could see him taking his place in any boardroom in the country.

She spoke at last, 'I didn't come to thank you, I came to return them. I do appreciate the thought—please don't think I'm entirely ungrateful—but—'

'What's wrong with them?'

'*Per se*, nothing. They're beautiful.' She ran her eyes over the lovely design and the leather of the bags. 'But they must have cost a small fortune.'

He shrugged. 'Quality can be expensive but a saving in the long run.'

Chas controlled a spurt of irritation and examined the intricate pattern of late-afternoon sunlight coming through the creeper-hung veranda onto the carpet.

'I do know that but Louis Vuitton to replace a pair of nylon bags? No, that's too much. I really couldn't accept them.'

He sat back and studied her. She wore a short jade leather skirt and a black sleeveless cotton-knit top. Her hair was shiny but tamed and tied back. Pity about that, he thought, and wondered what lovemaking would do to it. Create a glorious disarray?

Her light make-up was perfect, her golden skin was still amazingly clear and smooth. You'd probably have to be careful, he thought, not to mark or bruise her in bed.

She was also the essence of chic and the deep velvety blue of her eyes never failed to amaze him. Nor did the determined glint in them surprise him any longer.

OK, he thought with an inward grin, two can play this game. Let's see if I can surprise you, Chas Bartlett.

'You feel I might be trying to buy my way into your bed now?' he queried.

Her eyes widened.

'You know—' he clicked his fingers and went on before she could speak '—that honestly didn't occur to me but I apologise if that's how it looks. What I'll do is send them back and—you can choose a couple of appropriate bags that don't arouse any connotations of inappropriate behaviour on my behalf, and send me the bill.'

Her expression defied description for a moment.

Got you, Ms Bartlett, Tom thought with amusement, and proceeded to put the boot in.

'Well, since we've sorted that out, would you care to sit down and tell me how your plans are going?' he invited genially, then sobered with mock-wariness. 'But is even asking you to sit down in my study outside the bounds of appropriate behaviour from me?'

Chas clicked her tongue.

'Or,' he continued respectfully, 'could it be that you've deprived yourself of masculine company for so long it's beginning to tell? Making you cranky and so on?' he suggested chattily—and got ready to evade having his face slapped.

She surprised him. She hesitated briefly and clenched her fists, then she sank down opposite him. 'Probably,' she conceded. 'I'm not usually like this. That still doesn't mean the conventional solution is…' she glanced at him '…the *appropriate* one for me.'

Tom studied her, suddenly in a different mood altogether. 'Are you still in love with him?' he asked abruptly.

Chas considered. 'No.'

'That doesn't sound especially unequivocal,' he said with irony. 'Why did you call it off?'

'At the time, it occurred to me I was more in love with him than he was with me.'

'A week before the wedding?' He looked at her curiously.

'All the same.' Chas rubbed her fingertips along the edge of his desk. 'The closer we got to the wedding, the more I sensed that there was something missing between us. While we were greatly attracted, the emotional depths seemed to be all on my side. I've now revised my opinions, of course.'

'Of course,' he agreed with a touch of cynicism. 'How have you revised them?'

Chas smiled unexpectedly. 'You're expecting me to lay all the blame at his door, aren't you? I don't. It was the first time I'd ever thought I was in love, you see. I think…' She hesitated, then went on. 'I think I may have gone overboard, otherwise I would have realised there was an imbalance between us earlier.'

'So you see yourself as coming to your senses belatedly,' he said drily. 'But surely there must have been some kind of a catalyst?'

'There was. He had a woman in his past I didn't know about. He seemed quite sure he would be able to bury that past. I wasn't sure at all.'

'And you've since decided it was an aberration on your part, never to be repeated?'

She looked away. 'Until it happens to you, it may be hard to understand.'

He drummed his fingers on the desk.

'Look,' she said, 'I've told you this because to go on sparring with you and being so…so out of sorts with myself is upsetting me and unfair to you. But can we leave it there now?'

'Perhaps, but just tell me this. Why would Rupert, for example, and not myself—again, purely for example—' he looked ironic '—appeal to you if you're so turned off men?'

'Because you remind me of Rob,' she said simply. 'He was also good-looking, experienced, he attracted women in droves, and I'm told that falling in love with you is almost a national pastime.'

'Who told you that?'

'At least two people.'

He muttered something beneath his breath, highly uncomplimentary, she gathered from his expression.

She hid a smile and said serenely, 'Now that's sorted

out, would you like me to tell you how I've organised the retrieval of goodwill amongst your sister's wedding party?'

He gazed at her in so thoughtful a way, she got the nervous impression that she hadn't sorted anything out with him, but in the end all he said was, 'Why not?'

A day later only Harriet, Clare, Tom and Chas were left in residence at Cresswell Lodge. Vanessa, Rupert and his parents winged their way to Hayman Island and the Great Barrier Reef, and Chas began to work on her plan to include Harriet more in the wedding preparations.

'Mrs Hocking,' she began.

'Do call me Harriet, Chas!'

Chas smiled. 'Harriet, the long-range weather forecast is good for the wedding but they're never infallible, those forecasts, so perhaps we should think rain just in case it does pour.'

'Very wise,' Harriet agreed. 'But with the marquee we should be fine.'

'It's getting *to* the marquee I'm a bit worried about,' Chas said. 'One open carriage for the bride and groom, to be replaced by a limo if it rains, is not so difficult. Three open carriages might be a bit much, and, although it's such a lovely idea, I'm worried…' She broke off. 'What do you think?'

Harriet heaved a sigh. 'You're right. It would be chancy in wet weather. Even in fine weather, it had occurred to me it would perhaps take some of the emphasis off Vanessa and Rupert.'

Chas hesitated. 'I believe you thought of having some riders accompany the carriage?'

Harriet raised an eyebrow. 'You don't think it's a good idea either?'

'Not if they bring to mind fox-hunters,' Chas said honestly. 'It's a very touchy issue.'

'That's what Tom said. You could be right again.' Harriet looked thoughtful.

Chas wasted no time in pressing home her advantage. 'Now, there's an area where I really need your help, Harriet. The seating plan in the marquee. I think it's so important to get the right people together but, since I don't know any of them, I'm at a bit of a loss. I wondered if you and Clare would mind taking that over?'

'With pleasure,' Harriet enthused.

Chas dug into her briefcase and produced the plan for the marquee and she and Harriet discussed optimum table sizes and so on. She also showed Harriet one of the lovely little silver horse shoes she'd found to use as place-card holders and upon which she'd had engraved 'Rupert and Vanessa'.

'The guests can keep them as mementoes of the wedding,' she explained. Harriet was entranced.

A productive session, Chas decided, as once again she went in search of the master of Cresswell. With over a hundred guests the seating plan could take anyone days to sort out; it might just take Harriet and Clare a lot longer.

This time she found him down at the stallion barn. It was another lovely day and she thoroughly enjoyed her stroll up and down the drive towards the business end of Cresswell Lodge. Bees hummed in the flower beds beside the drive, dragonflies hovered and the air was so clear it shimmered.

The stallion barn, beneath its lovely little cupola,

faced onto a lawn. There were colourful tubs of flowering plants dotted along the paved walkways, and Tom Hocking was parading a huge, testy-looking, glossy brown horse for a small group of people.

Chas sat down on the wall that surrounded the lawn and took in the scene.

She'd already decided that the lawn, with the historic barn and cupola in the background, would be a perfect place for wedding photos, and that from there the bride and groom could transfer from their limo to the carriage for their triumphant drive to the homestead.

Now she looked at it with other eyes.

Cresswell stood six stallions, she'd learnt during her several visits. They also stood their own mares, but when the season commenced a stream of outside mares would be arriving at Cresswell, many with new foals at foot.

While she was thinking about all this, she was spotted by Brendan and Adam Baxter and they came over for a chat. She'd been introduced to Adam and his extremely grateful mother. When the boys left her, she turned her attention back to Tom.

What really intrigued her was the mastery Tom exercised over the stallion he was parading. The horse was obviously a reluctant participant in the proceedings. It showed a tendency to rear; it snorted and pawed the ground; it took off at one stage in a high-stepping circle around Tom with its tail extended like a banner, and Chas held her breath.

Would Tom be able to hold it?

Tom was able to, but she got the feeling it was a mental exercise as much as a physical one—almost as if he was saying to the horse: OK, have a bit of a fling but I'll decide when enough is enough.

The horse came to a standstill, and accepted a pat on the neck. The small crowd applauded discreetly, and the recognition slammed into Chas, almost taking her breath away, that she'd been floating on a cloud of false confidence.

She might have persuaded Tom Hocking that she was a lost soul, but she most definitely wasn't. Everything about this man filled her senses with appreciation and a growing longing.

There was that hint of arrogance and a certain tilt of his head—she'd seen it only moments ago—that told you he was clever and powerful and not to be taken lightly, but there was often humour, too, and it was a heady mix.

There was also, she thought, that certain something she couldn't read at all about him, as if there was a man within the man very few would be allowed to approach. As if there was more to the good-looking, highly capable, often casual boss of Cresswell—but what?

Then there were those good looks and his physique. The set of his shoulders, the power of his legs, just his hand drumming on a desk did strange things to her.

It was no good telling herself he reminded her of Rob, or that there was still the issue of Holly Maguire to be taken into consideration, let alone the unknown Sarah Oldfield. It was no good contemplating that a woman in his past might make him as intrinsically unreachable as Rob had been.

None of that changed the fact that she liked the challenge he often represented—even when she was arguing with him and trying to point out the error of his ways to him, she felt more alive than she had for a while. At other times she enjoyed his company, and, like the present, the mental strength as well as the physical strength he showed made her actually break out in goose-pimples like a silly girl.

Yet she'd strolled down to the stallion barn with every intention of telling him she was going back to Brisbane, firmly convinced that she was quite entitled to do so and it was what she wanted.

Only to discover in the blink of an eye that she'd been quite wrong.

Where the small white dog that created considerable havoc came from, she had no idea at the time. Later, she discovered that it had been left in one of the visitor's cars, tied by a flimsy lead to a door handle. All the car windows had been left open. The dog had chewed through the lead, jumped out of the car and, with yaps of ecstatic relief, streaked towards its owner on the lawn.

The stallion went berserk but it wasn't it that did the damage.

A stable hand leading another horse happened to be passing by. It also went berserk and pulled free of its handler.

Chas turned to see a horse galloping straight at her, and only had a moment to take evasive action. She threw herself sideways, hit her head on something, and everything went dark.

She came to in someone's arms.

'I was going to Brisbane,' she mumbled, 'and—'

'You're going nowhere,' a hard voice contradicted. 'Let me have a look at you.'

Chas blinked and squinted upwards. She was surrounded by a sea of anxious faces. Tom Hocking, the owner of the hard voice, added, 'Give us some air!'

The ring of faces receded and Chas discovered he was kneeling on the grass beside her, holding her in his arms.

'I'm sure I'm quite OK.' She licked her lips. 'How are the horses?'

'Fine. Are you hurting anywhere?'

'No. Well…' She touched her head with her fingertips, and winced.

Tom followed the path of her fingers with his own. 'A bump like an egg,' he said, 'but that's to be expected; you hit your head on the wall. Let's see if you can stand up.'

He helped her upright slowly and she stood for a moment then started to crumple. He picked her up with a muttered oath, and strode over to the stud office with her, issuing orders over his shoulder so that all interested spectators faded away.

She'd never been into the stud office but amongst all the other paraphernalia it contained there was an old settee. Tom closed the door with his foot and started to put her down on it.

She made a protesting sound, and he hesitated and looked down into her eyes.

'This feels better,' she whispered.

It took a moment for her meaning to sink in, then he sat down on the settee and kept her in his arms.

'Sorry,' she added and licked her dry lips, 'but I feel safe—or something like that. As if no stray horses with flying hooves can get me.' And she laid her head against his arm with a sigh of relief.

Something flickered in his eyes. He said, 'I don't have a problem with it but, Chas, I need to find out if there's anything else other than a bump on the head.'

'There isn't. I'm sure nothing is broken, I don't have

any internal aches and pains, just a really collywobbly feeling. Did the horse stand on me or anything like that?'

'It didn't touch you.'

'Did you lose control of the stallion?'

'No, which was a miracle.'

'Oh, I don't think so,' Chas murmured.

He grimaced. 'Thanks, but it could have been a whole lot worse. People and their damn dogs. In fact, though, you're the only one injured. Even the dog escaped.'

'I don't think I am injured. I'll probably be able to prove it to you in a moment.' She thought for a bit. 'I know who I am, where I am, who you are, and I can even give you my date of birth. And I don't have double vision or anything like that.'

'Good. There's no real hurry, then.'

'None at all.' She closed her eyes and rested against him for a couple of minutes in silence. It was like a haven against the images that had flooded her mind, of a horse galloping towards her, its lead rope dangling, its eyes white-rimmed with fear and its nostrils scarlet and distended.

She sighed gratefully as those images started to fade. As they did, it occurred to her that her growing feeling of well-being had a lot more to do with the man in whose arms she lay than the absence of scary mental pictures.

She lifted her lashes and discovered him staring at her mouth.

'It would be the height of folly for us to—get any closer,' she breathed.

He looked into her eyes and his lips quirked. 'Sometimes folly is hard to resist.'

'Yes, but I don't part with my convictions easily.'

'I had gathered that. On the other hand, rather than folly, it might be a perfectly natural impulse.'

A faint frown knitted her brow. 'You mean if I want you to kiss me and you want to do it, that makes it fine?'

He shrugged. 'It usually is—there's only one way to find out.'

'But the aftermath? I wouldn't want you to assume anything.'

'I won't,' he promised. 'Do you always talk these kind of moments to death?'

She bit her lip.

'Still…' He smiled suddenly. 'A bit of talk from me mightn't go astray.' He trailed his fingers down her bare arm. 'I love the feel of your skin, it's so smooth. I've sometimes wondered whether I would need to be extra careful in case I bruised you, which would be a shame. Then there are your eyes; I don't think I've ever seen such a deep blue but they can be—' he looked rueful '—extremely cool and determined.'

'I met you in the kind of circumstances that would—should!—make any girl a bit cool.'

His lips twitched. 'Be that as it may, is it really my fault that I happen to know how divinely put together you are?'

'I didn't think I was so…' She broke off and hesitated.

'You're gorgeous, Chas. And don't let *any* man make you feel otherwise. But that's enough talk.' He gathered her closer and rested his mouth on hers.

'I—'

'Shhh…' he admonished. 'Let's see if actions speak louder than words.'

*   *   *

Harriet Hocking got belated word of the fiasco at the stallion barn, and she raced down to see how Chas was and if she could help.

When told that Tom had Chas in the stud office she, perhaps fortunately, squinted through the window before she flung open the door.

It wasn't that easy to see in. There was a table piled high with books, papers and two large pot plants obscuring the view, but something made Harriet crane her neck and the sight she finally deciphered caused her to stop as if shot. Her son and the wedding consultant were engaged in a passionate embrace.

Her eyes widened, her jaw dropped, then she swung on her heel and raced back towards the homestead.

Clare was waiting anxiously for word on the veranda.

'How is she? Is she hurt? Did they call an ambulance?'

'No! I think she must be fine. I'm sure she must be fine because Tom is kissing her witless. Oh, Clare!' Harriet took her sister-in-law's hands joyfully. 'I had a sneaking little suspicion this might be on the cards! Maybe, just maybe, Chas Bartlett is the one Tom's been looking for all along!'

'Oh, dear,' Clare Hocking said slowly. 'Oh, dear, oh, dear!'

'What?' Harriet demanded. 'I thought you liked her?'

'I do. It's just a pity no one tells me anything.'

'Tells you what? We *do* but sometimes you're tuned right out!'

'Nobody told me about their sneaking suspicions,'

Clare protested, looking injured. 'If they had I wouldn't have done it.'

Harriet combined annoyance and apprehension rolled into one. 'What have you done now, Clare?'

'Well, Sarah Oldfield just rang. She's in the district—would you believe she's divorced?—and she wanted to pop in and see us. She was a dear girl even if she and Tom split up, you must admit. So I invited her to stay the night. It's not as if we don't have the space at the moment.'

Harriet closed her eyes. 'How could you? If nothing else,' she said through her teeth, 'you should have consulted Tom first! What am I going to *do*? Did she leave a phone number?'

'No. I don't think there's anything you can do, Harriet. You know, Sarah and Tom may just be good friends now.'

'Or Sarah may have realised she made an awful mistake and may be wanting to rectify things!'

Tom lifted his head at last.

Chas blinked and moved luxuriously in his arms.

'Was that something else or was that—something else?' he queried with a gleam in his grey eyes as he cradled her slim body.

'That was something else,' she agreed, with her breasts rising and falling rapidly beneath the silk of her blouse.

'How's the bump on your head?'

'What bump?'

He grinned wickedly. Chas trembled. She'd lost herself completely in his arms and beneath his kiss. Desire had coursed through her body, set alight by the feel and the taste of him. It had never felt so right to be touched and caressed, moulded and made to feel just like Aphrodite...

She blushed.

He raised an enquiring eyebrow as he followed the warm tide of colour rising to her cheeks.

'I had a strange thought, that's all.'

He circled her mouth with his thumb. 'Tell me.'

'I don't think I should.'

He moved his hand and let it hover over the buttons of her blouse. 'There's ways and means, lady,' he said out of the side of his mouth.

Her lips curved but she responded gravely. 'It's all your fault actually.'

'It usually is, between us.' He looked wry.

A silent jolt of laughter caught Chas unawares. 'Have I been that bossy?'

'At times.'

'I don't agree. That is, there've been times when you've gone out of your way to annoy me, then you've put me in place pretty thoroughly!'

He smiled and dropped a kiss on her forehead. 'Perhaps we've moved on to a new stage. So what was it?'

She looked perplexed.

'Why did you blush like that? I can't recall anything I did that would account for it, out of the blue like that, anyway.' He rubbed his jaw with his knuckles.

'A certain phrase came to mind,' she said cautiously. 'Alias Aphrodite.'

'Ah!' Enlightenment smote him. 'The goddess of love and beauty. Well. Tell you what—didn't she rise out of the sea on a shell?'

'Yes.'

'Thought so. And you may not know this, but there's a pool in the creek where we often swim. It's deep, it's private and there's a sandy bottom. We could do a bit of—classical recreation.'

Chas took her bottom lip between her teeth as she visualised herself rising out of a pool of water naked and dripping. Then she took a ragged breath and felt a dew of sweat break out on her spine as he drew a hand slowly down her body.

'All pink and gold, maybe creamier in some places the sun doesn't see,' he said barely audibly. 'But entirely delicious.'

'Whereas you,' her voice caught in her throat, 'would be brown and essentially masculine.' She broke off abruptly and tried to struggle upright.

'Hang on,' he said quietly. 'There's nothing wrong in fantasising together. Not after the way I kissed you and you kissed me.'

'No, but let's not go too fast,' she said rapidly, 'and there's someone coming!'

This time he did let her go and she scrambled off his lap.

Harriet Hocking made her presence felt with quite a bit of noise on her second visit. She allowed her heels to clack on the paving. She called out greetings to the horses stabled on either side of the stud office, then she rapped on the door and called Tom's name.

'Come in, Mother,' Tom replied. They were both present and—almost—correct. Chas was still attempting to smooth her hair.

'Chas!' Harriet came in. 'Are you all right? You look a bit shell-shocked but I'm not surprised from what I heard.' She swung to her son. 'How is she?'

'I think she's fine,' Tom said, 'but it wouldn't hurt for her to take things easy for a while.'

'Oh, definitely! Come up to the house, Chas, and let

me mother you a little. You could have concussion for all we know. Uh—Tom, I need to speak to you.'

'Fire away!'

'No, not now.'

'Beloved,' Tom said impatiently and drummed his fingers on the desk, 'I have a million things to do before dinner so it's now or never.'

Harriet gritted her teeth. 'Very well! Clare has invited Sarah Oldfield to spend the night with us.' She turned to Chas. 'You don't know her, my dear, and anyway, you might not feel up to meeting anyone so—'

'I'm fine,' Chas broke in, and thought swiftly. 'I think I really am but...' She hesitated. 'Anyway, I'll come up to the house with you now.'

Harriet stood irresolute but, since her son was eyeing her with a perfectly murderous glint in his eyes, she took the easy option. 'Let's go! I brought the car this time.' She broke off and bit her lip but neither Tom nor Chas appeared to notice the slip.

'Mrs Hocking—'

'Harriet.'

'Harriet,' Chas started again, 'what I was all set to do, and still think I'm fine to do, is drive back to Brisbane for a few days.'

'No way! Tom would shoot me if nothing else and he's not too...' Harriet broke off.

'But there's no reason for me to stay and, honestly, I also have a million things to do!'

'Chas...' Harriet swung the wheel. 'In all conscience I cannot allow you to drive yourself back to Brisbane, nearly a two-hour drive, after hitting your head on a wall and knocking yourself out! You must see that.'

'But...' They breasted the rise and Chas paused as

she noted the silver BMW parked on the drive, a car she didn't recognise.

'Ah. Sarah's already arrived by the look of it,' Harriet remarked with a note of helplessness that was quite foreign to her. 'If only Clare stopped to think occasionally…but there you go. Don't mind me, Chas.'

Sarah Oldfield was gorgeous, naturally. She was also blonde.

Arnold had provided a late-afternoon tea so Harriet and Chas sat down with Clare and Sarah at the veranda table, where Chas made other discoveries to do with Sarah Oldfield.

She had green eyes, she was tall and stylish with a sumptuous figure, she was warm and friendly. She was also very interested in Chas, and Vanessa's wedding, and she was aghast to hear how close Chas had come to being run down by a horse.

'I'm going to suggest she has a rest very shortly,' Harriet said, 'but in the meantime some nice warm tea won't hurt a bit. So, Sarah, what are you doing in this part of the world?'

Sarah hesitated and lowered her eyes briefly, and Chas took an unexpected breath. There was no doubting a moment of sadness or pain had clouded those green eyes before Sarah Oldfield looked down that reminded Chas acutely of—who?

'Just visiting,' Sarah said quietly.

It hit Chas suddenly. Holly Maguire.

But hadn't Sarah married someone else? Yet there were no rings on her left hand, and why was she at Cresswell, anyway? Why, come to that, was Harriet in a bit of a fluster? Could Sarah be attempting a reunion with Tom, thoughtlessly encouraged by Clare before

Harriet had had a chance to discover where her son stood on the subject?

That was when it occurred to Chas that she had a headache and she felt a bit sick. Entirely due to hitting her head on a wall and knocking herself out?

Or was it at least compounded by being confronted by another old flame of Tom's who couldn't forget him?

Maybe I'm imagining it all, she told herself, but her mind fastened on something Harriet had said. *If only Clare stopped to think...*

She shook her head and decided she had to extricate herself, and the only way to do that was plead a reaction and take herself to bed.

This caused a flurry of concern but finally she was alone in the cream bedroom, having given every firm indication that that was where she intended to stay.

Thankfully, she thought as she hugged herself, no one had any idea why Sarah Oldfield would be such a revelation to her. But was she right about the pain and sadness she'd seen in Sarah's eyes? And was it to do with Tom?

CHAPTER SEVEN

CHAS woke at three o'clock the next morning, having slept, to her amazement, for about ten hours straight.

There was evidence on her bedside table of Harriet, she presumed, coming in to visit her. There was a sandwich and some biscuits in a lunch box, and a small Thermos of coffee.

She attended to a call of nature and discovered that her headache had vanished. So had the nausea. She took herself back to bed and propped herself up against the pillows. She ate the sandwich, egg and lettuce, and drank the coffee.

It crossed her mind that Harriet Hocking would make a nice mother-in-law.

She immediately looked ceiling-ward and asked herself what on earth she could be thinking. Then she decided she had no idea what to think. She was confused, she was feeling extremely wary—as if she'd walked into a minefield, in fact—and she needed, at least, to regroup.

She got up, showered and dressed, and went to pack, then remembered that she had nothing to pack into. She hadn't replaced her bags; it had slipped her mind.

'Damn!' she muttered but her gaze fell to the floor of the built-in wardrobe, and the two Louis Vuitton bags sitting neatly side by side.

Someone—it had to be on Tom's express instructions—had returned the bags to her room. She muttered something beneath her breath and yanked them out.

Just before she left, she wrote a note thanking the Hockings for their kindness, assuring them she was fine now but, since she'd woken early, she'd decided to take advantage of it and drive back to Brisbane for a few days.

She stole out of the house, made a discreet fuss of Leroy and Piccanin, and drove away just as a hint of dawn lightened the darkness.

The silver BMW was still parked on the drive.

Chas loved her apartment.

It overlooked the Brisbane river and the building had once been a wool store. Its metamorphosis into an apartment building had retained the heritage aspect of the outer building; there were several of them and they were beloved landmarks on the river. But inside it was high-ceilinged and spacious. She'd converted the guest bedroom into a studio.

She often watched the river traffic, the barges, the ferries, the yachts and cruisers, the early-morning rowing teams, the seagulls.

She spent two hours at her desk, clearing a backlog of mail, and relishing the way she was instantly enveloped by a much safer feeling. She was on her home ground.

She answered her front-door bell, convinced it would be her mother, whom she'd rung to say she was home and invited for a cup of coffee on her way to work if she had the time. Instead, it was Tom.

'How—how—' she took a step backwards, her eyes dilating '—how did you get here? So soon, I mean. I mean…' She trailed off.

'I do own an airline.' He eyed her hair, caught up

in a wide-tooth comb clip. He eyed the short, silky halterneck shift she wore, and her bare feet.

Chas moved uneasily. 'I left a note—I'm fine!'

'So you said. Do you make a habit of kissing men, talking about Aphrodite and bolting?' he queried.

Chas was lost for words.

He took her hand off the door, picked her up at the waist and carried her inside so he could step over the doorstep and closed the door behind him. 'I smell coffee—I could do with it.'

Chas came to life. 'No, I don't make a habit of that, but bumping into your ex-lovers does seem to be habit-forming!'

'Sarah? Who told you that? Clare? My mother?' He frowned then shrugged. 'Not that it matters.' He turned her around and propelled her towards the source of the coffee aroma.

'Will you stop manhandling me, Tom Hocking?' She wrested herself from his grasp and marched into the kitchen.

'Nice view,' he commented.

She took the coffee-pot off the stove and poured coffee into two colourful mugs. 'Help yourself.' She pointed to the milk jug and sugar bowl. 'There's an even better view in here.' Her voice was strictly neutral.

He followed her into the lounge.

She'd decorated it in fawns, sherbet green and dusky pink.

'Do sit down.'

He chose a sherbet armchair. She perched herself in the corner of the pink velvet settee.

'I was coming back,' Chas said carefully. 'I wasn't

planning to abandon Vanessa's wedding or anything like that.'

'Good. But that's not the point.'

Chas studied him. As well as flying down to Brisbane he'd found time to shave, and he wore pressed jeans and a check shirt with polished short boots.

She put her mug on the coffee-table. 'I felt as if I'd strayed into a minefield. You must admit that bumping into *two* women you'd been…' she hesitated '…*associated* with is enough to make anyone wonder.'

'Wonder what?'

'You know.' She gestured.

'If I'm some kind of Bluebeard?'

'Not exactly, but all the same…' She searched for words. 'They both looked sad.'

'Chas, I don't know if whoever told you about Sarah also told you that she left me for another man, a man she married?'

'Yes, but is she still married to him?'

'No.' He drank some coffee. 'They're divorced. There's no question of Sarah and I getting back together, however.'

Chas had to smile. 'You sorted that out pretty quickly.'

'Yes. As for Holly Maguire…' He looked briefly into the distance. 'Did you know that what Holly was really madly in love with was marriage and security?'

Chas frowned. 'That's not the way she told it to me.'

'Nevertheless, it's true. Do you know her background?'

Chas thought for a moment. 'Not that much. I never met her family. Come to think of it, she hardly ever mentioned them.'

'She came from a broken home. She spent years in boarding-schools. When her mother died she moved into her father's home but didn't get on with his second wife, and she felt second best to his other children. All of it left her with terrible insecurities.' He grimaced. 'But until you probed a bit deeper beneath that bubbly personality, you would never know it.'

Chas stared at him.

'She clung,' he said slowly, 'in a way that was no more good for her than it was for me.'

Chas knitted her fingers. 'She's taken it so hard, though.'

'I hate to say this but Holly is her own worst enemy. If we'd gone on any longer, she would have been even more hurt.'

Chas shook her head. 'Then you let it go on for too long, otherwise surely she'd have got over it by now.'

'Is a few weeks too long?'

Chas gasped. 'That's all?'

He nodded and his lips twisted. 'It may interest you to know there's been no one since.'

Chas licked her lips. 'Why?'

'I may not have been the man for Holly but that doesn't mean to say I didn't regret the turmoil she went through.' He looked away for a moment. 'But I can guarantee this. She will fall in love again—I just hope with a man and not marriage and security *per se*, next time.'

Chas frowned. 'How can you be so sure that's what it was and not you?'

'Sex is one thing,' he said. 'A mental rapport is another. Once the initial attraction, ah, settled down, we hardly had anything in common.'

'So it left you with a bitter taste in your mouth?'

'Of course.' He looked at her with that arrogant tilt to his head.

She shrugged and sighed. 'I'm sorry. Was Sarah ever on your wavelength?'

'Look, that's old history. How would you feel if I insisted on knowing every quirk of every relationship you've had?'

'There aren't…' Chas stopped. *That many*, she'd been going to say, but said instead, 'I take your point. So where do we go from here?'

'The ball, ma'am—' a glint of humour entered his grey eyes '—is in your court.'

Chas got up and went over to the windows. After a long moment of thought, she said, 'Would you mind if I suggested we take things slowly?'

'No,' he replied, from right behind her.

She turned abruptly.

'Particularly as I'm on my way to New Zealand for a week, alias Aphrodite,' he said quietly, and put his hands on her waist.

'I don't think you should call me that,' she murmured.

He scanned her mouth and her breasts. 'No? Why not?'

'It…' She took a ragged breath as the devastating attraction of Tom Hocking washed over her. 'It doesn't matter. New Zealand! You didn't say anything about that.'

He looked satanically amused. 'I may not have got the chance.'

'So you didn't only come to see me this morning? Not that I…' She broke off in confusion.

'I certainly did come to see you this morning.'

'Yes, well…' Chas paused to gather her thoughts.

'Getting back to how we proceed, slowly is fine with me so long as we're honest.' He searched her eyes.

'Honest?' she breathed. 'I mean, I'm all for honesty at all costs, but—'

He cut her off and his hands moved down to her hips. 'Honest as in admitting to this at least—we want each other.'

'What about a mental rapport, though?' she queried.

'That's already in place. I really enjoy sparring with you, dear wedding consultant.' He looked down at her wryly. 'I think I'd rather argue with you than just about anyone else.'

Chas's eyes widened. 'If that's not—surely that's— well, isn't an argumentative relationship a minus?'

'Not at all,' he drawled. 'We stimulate each other.'

Chas bit her lip. It was true but…what?

'Think about it,' he advised. 'In the meantime I have to dash, but may I leave you with this, Ms Bartlett?'

'This' turned out to be an exercise that left Chas feeling she might as well have been taken to bed.

She wore no bra beneath her halterneck dress, only a skimpy pair of bikini briefs. He skimmed the outline of her figure from her armpits to the swell of her hips, drawing his thumbs down the valley between her breasts as his hands moved downwards.

The silky material of her dress rubbed sensuously against her skin and his hands on it made her conscious of every curve she possessed, every slender line; conscious of them and framed by his long, powerful hands, so that when he stopped doing it she was in some disarray.

Her breathing was tumultuous and her nipples had peaked beneath the flimsy silk. Her hair had started to fall out of the comb.

He removed the comb with an absent smile and cupped her face. 'I much prefer it loose rather than all the ways you've tried to tame it into submission lately.' He waited for a moment then smiled into her eyes. 'What—no feisty retort?'

'I... It must be too early in the morning.'

'What if I do this?' he queried and slid his fingers round to the back of her neck. The knot of her halter top flicked undone.

Chas did her best to tell him to stop but she was well and truly mesmerised by the sensations he'd aroused in her as well as by his tanned, powerful body, his shoulders and the whole masculine effect of him that she was, or so it seemed, drinking in through every pore.

Her lips trembled, her eyes widened as the top slipped down to reveal her pink-tipped breasts, but it was only pleasure she was conscious of as he cupped them and played with her nipples. Pure physical pleasure, and a mental delight at the way she was his feminine counterpart in those moments, and affecting him as much as he was affecting her.

She could see it in the way his eyes darkened, the way his breathing altered and his hand became more urgent.

Then he stopped and looked into her eyes again. 'New Zealand,' he said, 'is going to be pure hell.' And he put his arms around her and kissed her deeply.

Then he put her away from him, did up her halter-neck and touched a fingertip to her ripe mouth. 'Look after yourself till I get back. When do you plan to go back to Cresswell?'

'I— You— When Vanessa returns,' she said disjointedly.

'Thanks!' He leant down and kissed her again, but this time with the lightest touch, and he left.

Chas stood like a statue until she tottered to the settee and sank down, prey to a whole host of conflicting emotions.

You needed a licence to deal with Tom Hocking, was one of her thoughts, a sort of dangerous-goods handling licence.

But when the reaction to his kiss, and everything else he'd done to her, subsided somewhat, she found her thoughts returning to Holly Maguire. And it occurred to her that Holly had been a rather possessive friend; quick to be jealous of other friends then, as if to cover it, at her lively, sparkly best.

Why didn't I remember that? she wondered. But it did make sense of Tom's version, now she came to think of it.

She sighed and looked down at her hands. Putting aside Holly and Sarah Oldfield, the real question was, what future did she see for herself and Tom Hocking?

Her mother came for lunch rather than coffee.

'How's this wedding going?' Hope Bartlett asked as they ate the sandwiches she'd brought with her and drank iced tea. 'The one that keeps taking you to—Warwick, is it?' Hope was in her fifties but still strikingly elegant.

'Almost Warwick.' Chas wiped her mouth with a napkin and reached for her tea glass. 'It's like a minefield.' She described some of the goings-on.

'Heavens above! You're a braver man than I am, Gunga Din.' Hope chuckled. 'It could be marvellous advertising for you, though!'

'That's the only reason I persevered,' Chas said with some irony. 'How's Dad?' she asked.

'Fine. Well, I think he's doing a bit too much at the moment. I just wish he could delegate, but you know your father.'

Chas nodded. She adored her father, but there was no way she could visualise him ever voluntarily slowing down. In fact she adored both her parents, and she was full of admiration for their loving relationship.

She thought about that for a moment, then she said slowly, 'Mum, is an argumentative relationship with a man a sign of some rapport?'

Hope Bartlett narrowed her eyes and wondered if her daughter was, at last, recovering from the late cancellation of her wedding. 'I suppose it could be,' she said slowly. 'Depends what you argue about, how deeply the disagreements go, or if it's a kind of verbal sparring that is stimulating. Why?'

'Rob and I hardly ever argued.'

'Are you still…finding it hard to get over, Chas?'

Chas frowned. 'I guess it's the after-effects I'm stuck with.'

Hope heaved a sigh. 'To be honest, both your father and I thought he was a bit—' she gestured with a beringed hand '…oh, charming, funny, very likeable, but perhaps not capable of as deep a commitment as you were.'

'As it turned out, he was capable of it but not to me. How do you know I'm capable of "deep commitment"—if I am?' Chas asked.

'Chas, since you were a little girl you've given everything to everything you've undertaken.' Hope waved a hand. 'Look at the success you've made of this business.'

Chas looked around. 'Just occasionally,' she confessed, with a tinge of surprise, 'I'd like to try my hand at something else.'

'Why not? I don't doubt that anything else you took on would prosper. What kind of thing?'

'I don't know!' Chas laughed. 'Up until a few moments ago I thought I was very happy with weddings but I don't—I don't know, I feel a bit restless at the moment. But, Mum, getting back to Rob, why didn't I see that until it was almost too late?' she asked intensely.

'Darling, to be honest, you left it rather late to fall in love for the first time. And that's a situation when not many of us are pillars of wisdom.' Hope shrugged. 'You may even start to wonder if there's something wrong with you.' She looked at her daughter keenly.

'I was about the only one in my circle who hadn't had several love affairs.' Chas spread her hands.

'Well, that can flaw your judgement. Has someone come into your life?'

'Rather like a torpedo,' Chas said darkly. 'I argue with him virtually all the time! I'm unbelievably bossy, I put my foot in where angels would *die* rather than tread and—and he claims it indicates a mental rapport!'

'He could be right,' Hope said slowly. 'Who is he?'

'But the other problem is,' Chas continued, 'we may enjoy sparring with each other but there's a side of him I feel I don't know at all and that reminds me of Rob. I also think…' She paused and frowned as the thought hit her. 'I think it's a problem other women may have run into as well. Oh, it's—it's the bride's brother.'

Hope's eyes widened. 'Quite a catch by the sound of it.'

'Mum!'

Hope chuckled. 'Sorry. Um, perhaps you'd be well-advised to stand no nonsense from the bride's brother.'

Chas's mind flew back a couple of hours. 'Easier said than done.' She looked rueful. 'In more ways than one!'

'Chassie,' her mother said thoughtfully, 'I think the lesson you needed to learn from the Rob fiasco was— so you made some mistakes, you took some wrong readings, but we all do, and, hopefully, we learn from them. But so far as Rob misleading you as he did…' Hope hesitated. 'It would be another mistake to think all men are the same.'

'That's what he said, the bride's brother.'

'He's right, darling. Would there be any chance of me getting to meet him?'

Chas heaved a sigh. 'I'll see. Maybe after the wedding. If we're still, well, you know.'

After her conversation with her mother, Chas brooded a bit on the after-effect of her called-off wedding she'd told no one about: the feeling that she might not be much good in bed.

She also pondered briefly on the conviction that had come to her while talking to her mother—that both Holly and Sarah Oldfield, and others for all she knew, might have found it hard to get through to the real Tom Hocking.

Fortunately she had enough work on hand to be able to close off her mental musings when she decided she was going round in circles, so instead she concentrated on getting two other weddings to the altar as well as the Weaver-Hocking one.

At the same time, however, her new, odd feeling of restlessness touched her in the form of an unbidden thought along the lines of: Shouldn't there be more to life than organising weddings?

Of course, she was honest enough to admit, part of her success lay with her attention to detail and the time she took to handle the people involved as well. But it was terribly time-consuming, wasn't it? Could she say, for example, that she had a life away from weddings?

She was back at Cresswell when Vanessa, Rupert and his parents came back from the Barrier Reef. Tom was still in New Zealand.

Their glowing expressions told their own story. All injury at the venue for the wedding seemed to be forgotten. Vanessa was looking particularly relaxed.

She even confronted Chas with sparkling amusement. 'I can't believe you did this!'

'What have I done now?' Chas asked humorously.

'It's not that, not as if you have a history of making trouble—it's the opposite. But asking Mum and Clare to organise the seating plan was asking for trouble! It's little short of war.'

'Oh, dear. I did hope it might take them a while,' she explained. 'I didn't mean to start a war.'

'Let's you and I do it together now,' Vanessa suggested.

So they set themselves up in Tom's study and closed the door.

While she had Vanessa to herself, Chas ran through everything to do with the wedding at the same time.

'The marquee is going up the day before but the company is supplying a man to stand by on the day, in case of any difficulties—can we put the Smiths with the Walkers?'

'Yep. They're lovely old fuddy-duddies and they adore a good gossip.'

'Right.' Chas continued down her mental list until she came to the wedding party. 'Don't forget we're having a trial run this Saturday of make-up and hairdos as well as the final fitting for the dresses.'

Vanessa nodded. 'The bridesmaids are organised. I'm getting excited,' she added.

'Good.' Chas beamed at her. 'What else? Oh, Tom, Rupert, the best man and the ushers need to have a trial run of their suits, too. That's something I haven't managed to organise yet.'

'Rupe and the ushers I may be able to leg-rope.' Vanessa grinned. 'But the best man doesn't fly in from England until next week. And Tom…we'll just have to do the best we can. Mind you, he's been pretty good lately.'

'I think he does have your best interests at heart.'

Vanessa propped her chin on her hand. 'I know. The thing with Tom is, he never expected to be tied down to Cresswell so soon.'

Chas frowned. 'What do you mean?'

'I think he finds it pretty frustrating at times.'

'What…what would he have been doing otherwise?'

'Didn't you know?'

Chas shook her head.

Vanessa looked around then she got up and lifted a framed photo down from the mantelpiece. 'That's his real love,' she said. 'Benindee.'

Chas stared down at the photo. Tom was standing beside a light plane, shading his eyes from the sun as he gazed over a vast plain dotted with trees and scored with gullies.

'It's a cattle station on Cape York. It's been in the

family for generations but it got run down and virtually abandoned. When he came out of the air force he decided to rescue it. He's always loved it up there.'

'So did he rescue it?'

'He started to,' Vanessa said. 'Then Dad got ill so he came home. I think he stayed because of me and Mum after Dad passed away—far too young,' Vanessa said sadly. 'Cresswell means so much to us but neither she nor I were the least good at running it. It's not only Cresswell,' she added. 'It's quite an empire but I guess Cresswell is the flagship.'

'Could he put in managers?' Chas suggested.

'I think he probably will one day. It's funny, though. He lost Sarah Oldfield because of Benindee, she didn't want to be stuck out the back of beyond. I believe you met her?'

'Yes, I did.'

'Well, she's divorced and if Mum is to be believed she's trying to make a go of it with Tom again.' Vanessa shook her head and put the picture back. 'Anyway, if Tom seems prickly at times, that's why.'

'There you go.'

Chas closed herself into the cream bedroom she'd been allotted again, after she and Vanessa had finished the seating plan, and leant against the door. She was now alone in the homestead apart from the staff. Everyone else had gone to a cocktail party on a neighbouring property. This time she'd successfully evaded being dragooned into attending herself.

Tom Hocking in a nutshell?

No, she doubted it.

She moved away from the door and went over to the window.

But at least some things made more sense now. At least it explained the man within the man, the man with a different agenda. The man, now she came to think about it, she could no longer classify as a serial womaniser, and not only from discovering this new side to him but also because she'd observed no signs of it during the past weeks.

How did it help her?

Hard to say, she mused. Then her eyes widened as Leroy flashed past the window with Piccanin hot on his heels. Leroy had something large in his mouth.

Suddenly mindful of the destruction of her bags and that she might be the only one around, she ran from her room onto the veranda and chased around the corner of the house after the dogs, only to run full tilt into Tom.

'Whoa!' Somehow he saved them both from falling over.

'Chas! Does this mean you really missed me?'

'No,' she panted. 'I mean…I mean, I'm glad to see you back, but Leroy has something in his mouth and the destruction of it on his mind, I'm quite sure, so—'

He put a finger to her lips. 'It's sorted.'

'How can it be sorted? It was only moments ago!'

'It's a bone. We've finally trained him not to excavate the garden while burying his bones, so he's off to the paddock.'

Chas blinked several times as her breathing settled down. 'It must have been a huge bone.'

'He's a very large dog. How are you?'

'I'm fine.' She looked up at him. 'How was New Zealand?'

'Very kiwi.' He grinned and took her hand. 'Care for a little walk?'

'If you've only just arrived,' she objected, 'don't you want to—'

'No, I don't. So—'

'You don't know what I was about to say!'

'It doesn't matter. All I want is to be somewhere private with you.' His grey eyes glinted.

'Oh.'

'There's a bench under the trees not far from here,' he added. 'I don't doubt you have some articulate thoughts on the matter, you usually do, but—'

'"Lay on, Macduff,"' she said gravely.

He laughed, and started to walk her towards the creek.

The bench was not that far away from the house but it was like another world.

The willow trees gave way to native gums, the lawn to scrub, there was a whip bird calling and the bench, on a patch of grass, overlooked a pool in the creek bed. The bank leading down to it was composed of rich dark soil but the pool had sandy edges and looked immensely inviting on what was a hot summer's day.

'This isn't…' Chas stopped.

'This is our swimming hole. I may have mentioned it.'

'You did,' Chas replied with a certain fatalism, and looked down at her cargo trousers and blouse. 'I'm not dressed for any classical recreation.'

'I don't think Aphrodite was dressed either but that's not what I had in mind, today. Sit down.'

She did. He sat beside her and stretched his arm out behind her.

'OK. What have you come up with while I've been selling yearlings in New Zealand, Dr Watson?' he queried, his grey eyes glinting.

Chas turned to look at him incredulously. 'What do you mean?'

He raised a satanic eyebrow. 'I thought you were engaged in unravelling all the mysteries to do with Thomas Hocking. His intentions, his prospects, his motivations, his history, whether he has his own teeth, how many peachy blondes have littered his path.'

Chas all but choked on the strangled sound she made. 'That's—'

'Not funny?' he suggested. 'Not true?'

'That's diabolical! Mind you, there's one thing I'm wondering. How he reacts to this.'

She kicked her sandals off, wriggled swiftly out of her trousers, flung off her blouse and, without a backward glance, climbed down the bank and waded into the creek.

The water was fresh, startlingly so. 'Wow!' she called. 'Only one way to do this!' She dived beneath the surface.

When she came up, Tom came up in front of her. His brown hair was plastered to his head, he'd discarded his shirt, but she couldn't see what else he'd discarded.

'Oh, no, you don't!' she sang out, and swam away like an eel.

It took him several energetic minutes to capture her, by which time they were both laughing and breathless.

'I hope you're at least partially presentable, Mr Hocking,' she quipped.

'Like you, Ms Bartlett,' he replied gravely but with a wicked glint, 'I've retained my undies—is that good enough? Whose idea was this, anyway?'

'Mine. Just a pity I couldn't see your face.'

He pulled her into his arms. 'I can tell you what it said—does this girl always have to have the last word?'

Chas dissolved into laughter. 'You must admit your attack was a bit below the belt.'

'So it hit home?' he hazarded.

Chas was standing on her toes, he was standing quite easily on the bottom with his shoulders above the water. They were smooth, brown and strong and it crossed her mind that she should swim away before she did anything silly.

Anything like laying her lips on them or the strong column of his throat, like winding her arms around his neck and kissing his mouth. But she knew immediately she had no chance of swimming away unless he let her.

'Yes, despite the humour of it, it hit home,' she conceded.

He looked into the deep blue of her eyes beneath the wet clumps of her lashes. 'At least we can laugh about it.'

'I don't know if we should, too much,' she said. 'Perhaps where it hit home is the rather obsessive side of me that's always looking for answers.'

What he would have replied to that she was not to know because Leroy crashed through the scrub at that moment, followed, of course, by Piccanin. They paused, surveyed the scene, and then, with a joyful volley of barks, both dogs plunged into the creek, Leroy, at least, creating a small tidal wave.

Chaos ensued for some minutes. Leroy leapt out of the water, rounded up Tom's shirt and jeans in his jaws and leapt back in again. Piccanin, not to be outdone, collected Chas's blouse and trousers and struggled manfully back into the water with them.

When Chas and Tom finally emerged, having rescued their clothes, she was spluttering and holding her side from too much laughter.

She dragged herself up the bank and flopped onto the bench. 'That's a crazy dog, you know,' she gasped. 'When he's not chewing up my possessions he's trying to drown me or my clothes! Don't say it,' she warned as Tom sat down beside her. 'He's little more than the biggest puppy I've ever seen!'

'Look out, here he comes,' Tom warned in turn. 'Prepare for another shower.'

Leroy rolled in some mud his tidal wave had created, then raced up the bank, planted himself in front of them and shook himself mightily. Chas took refuge in Tom's arms, laughing all the more.

'Oh, dear,' she whimpered at last when the dogs had taken themselves off. 'Do you think we're safe for a while?'

'Mmm…' He wiped a spray of mud from her cheek with his fingers. 'But not safe from this.'

She knew what was coming and made no attempt to avoid it. There was no way she could summon up any opposition to something that felt so right, so exquisite.

His fingers on her damp skin aroused tremors of delight. Her undies consisted of a matching set, a coffee-coloured lace bra and hipster briefs trimmed with ivory silk rosettes.

'Very sexy,' he said against the corner of her mouth and slid one bra strap aside to reveal her breast. The tight pink buds of her nipples unfurled again, just as they'd done when she'd first dived into the water, but this time in direct response to him.

He bent his head and teased the exposed nipple with his tongue.

Chas made a husky sound and arched her body over his encircling arm as the lovely sensations he aroused washed down her body. Then he sought her lips and she made another husky little sound as he kissed her and his fingers wrought further devastation. He slipped the wet lace of her briefs down and cupped each buttock.

Then he eased her off the bench so that they were kneeling on the patch of grass in front of it, facing each other, holding each other urgently. She was kissing him back and pressing her breasts against him as she nurtured that special delight he'd started for her, trying to return it, smoothing his shoulders, kissing his throat then returning to his mouth and cupping his jaw.

It was desperate and dizzy, as if they couldn't get enough of each other.

And all the time his fingers wandered over her skin and finally slid down to her thighs, hesitated briefly, then explored the warm, secret place between them.

Chas gasped as she was rocked by an explosion of rapture, and, to her amazement, she felt the same shudders rock him as he held her hard against his body.

Her lips parted incredulously and her eyes were wide as they stopped kissing each other and instead stared at each other.

She started to say something but couldn't formulate the words so she licked her lips cautiously instead.

He smiled fleetingly as their mutual shudders subsided to tremors. And it was only when they were still at last that he spoke, and demonstrated that he'd read the incredulous question in her eye. 'How could that have happened? We wanted each other rather badly, that's how. Come.'

He stood up and helped her to her feet and led her down to the pool again.

Daylight had almost faded as they waded in and floated side by side for a while, holding hands again.

Chas stared up at the last pink tinges of sunset in the sky above the trees and, for once in her life, was totally speechless as she contemplated the sheer mystery of certain things.

Such as how she'd laboured towards true fulfilment with a fiancé she'd thought she loved but never quite made it, only to be given it by a man she wasn't at all sure about, who hadn't actually taken her…

If Tom was aware of the momentous nature of her uncharacteristic silence, he gave no sign of it.

He helped her out, and they climbed the bank and got dressed with difficulty. Then they looked at each other. Their clothes were not only dripping wet but also liberally splattered with mud.

'We have two options,' he said gravely. 'We can go back into the pool fully clothed to wash the mud off; or we can go home muddy.'

A growing smile disturbed Chas's dazed expression.

'I don't think it makes much difference. No one's home.' She explained about the cocktail party.

'Muddy it is, then. Are you OK?'

'I'm… I'm stunned,' she said honestly.

He leant forward and kissed her very gently. 'I'm not so unaffected myself. What would you give for a drink and a quiet talk?'

'Quids.'

He laughed and they set off towards the house, but were to be thwarted in the matter of no one home, at least.

CHAPTER EIGHT

ABOUT a hundred metres from the house, where the trees met the lawn, Tom stopped and frowned.

Chas, in a little world of her own, looked up at him.

'It sounds to me as if they've brought the cocktail party home. Damn,' he said, with feeling.

'Is there any way we could slip around the back?'

His grip on her hand tightened. 'Too late. We've been spotted. You're right about that bloody dog.'

It was Leroy again, bounding across the lawn to greet them, and at least thirty people gathered on the veranda and the fringes of it turned to see whom he was greeting.

'Play it cool, lady,' Tom advised out of the side of his mouth.

'But I must look such a wreck,' Chas breathed.

He exerted pressure on her hand and turned her towards him. 'You look a million dollars, Aphrodite,' he said with his lips quirking. 'And if it's of any interest to you, that has never happened to me before.'

'Oh.'

'Hey, you two!' Vanessa called. 'We were wondering where you were! Come and join the party. We've decided to have a barbecue.'

They moved forward. 'Oh?' he repeated wryly.

'Well, maybe this isn't the time or place to go into that.'

'Coward,' he said softly, and they strolled into the circle of light from the veranda.

'Look here—no!' she protested, and was saved, in a way, by Vanessa, who came forward to greet them. 'Everybody who doesn't know him, meet my brother, Tom, and my wedding…' She stopped and her eyes widened. 'What on earth have you two been doing?'

'Swimming,' Tom drawled. 'It's very good for you. You should try it some time.'

'But—' Harriet came to the fore and also eyed them incredulously '—in your clothes? And what about the mud?'

'That was Leroy's idea of fun. Would you excuse us?' Tom said at large and with a charming smile. 'Have fun yourselves!' And he led Chas round the side of the house.

They both missed the highly taken-aback glance that simply shouted *Is this what I think it is?* that Vanessa bestowed upon her mother. They didn't see Clare pat her soft, rouged cheek and shake her head.

But through every pore of her body, Chas, at least, was conscious of the unspoken speculation she was on the receiving end of as she walked away. So much so that by the time they were out of sight her cheeks were red and her composure was sorely tried.

'Here's what I suggest,' Tom said with a grin as he scanned the signs of her discomfort. 'We'll go in through the laundry and discard our clothes. Then, after a shower, we could meet up in my study. I'll get Arnold to rustle us up a snack—you don't want to go to the party, do you?'

'No way!' Horror now added itself to the mixture of her expressions.

'Good.' He opened the laundry door. 'See you soon.'

Fortunately the cream bedroom wasn't far from the laundry and Chas encountered no one as she ran, in her bra and pants and a towel Tom had found for her, from the laundry to it.

She closed herself in with a sigh of relief and went straight to the shower.

When she sat down at the dressing table, she was clean and shining; she'd dried her hair and left it loose. But was there anything about her, she wondered, her eyes perhaps, the fluttery feeling that was making her a little clumsy, or any other outward sign that she had been translated?

Translated? She pondered the word that had sprung to mind. Maybe she meant transported? Whatever—she flipped her hand—surely she wouldn't be so un-*soignée* as to get around to actually showing it? She was twenty-six, after all.

Normally—here she grimaced at her reflection—she was pretty good at hiding her reactions. Then again, in relation to Tom Hocking, that was hardly the case and hadn't been since she'd climbed, uninvited, into his bed.

She took a quick, uncertain breath and saw her nostrils pinch with the effort to stay calm.

At the same time there was a light rap on her door and Tom called through the panels that their supper was ready.

'Coming!' she called back.

But she forced herself to sit still for another two minutes, and breathe deeply.

Their supper was on the coffee-table in front of the fireplace in Tom's study.

He'd pulled both armchairs up and there was an open bottle of champagne on the table.

'This is becoming a habit,' she murmured, as she accepted a glass from him.

'Cheers. A nice one. Take a seat.'

Chas did so and smoothed her long skirt around her knees. It was turquoise cotton with little white flowers, a comfortable and familiar item of clothing she often wore at home. With it she had on a lacy white knit top.

She inspected their supper, sandwiches and lidded cups of soup, then she lifted her gaze to Tom.

He was leaning against the mantelpiece. He'd changed into a dark blue linen shirt with the sleeves half rolled up and hanging loose over lighter blue canvas trousers. His feet were bare, his brown hair was still damp and he was gazing at the carpet.

She said suddenly, 'I don't know what to say.'

He lifted his eyes and there was amusement in them as well as something else she couldn't name.

'That's unusual.'

She bit her lip.

'Do we have to say anything?' he murmured. 'Although here's one thing—you look pretty.'

'I feel pretty. I mean, I feel pretty amazed,' she contradicted herself.

He set his glass down on the mantelpiece and came over to her. He took her glass away from her and drew her to her feet. 'Pretty enough to kiss, caress, cradle, explore, even ravish—assuming it was mutual,' he said barely audibly.

'I don't think there could be any doubt about that,' she whispered.

He put his hands on her hips.

Chas closed her eyes and rested against him. 'All the same, it could be a problem,' she breathed.

'How so, Miss Bartlett?' he queried, and kissed the top of her head.

'Well, I have a job to do. It's only about ten days to the wedding and things are bound to get a bit frantic. If I can't keep my hands off you, I'm going to be in trouble.'

She felt his jolt of laughter through her cheek. 'I'm the one with my hands on you,' he pointed out.

'Doesn't matter.' She glanced up into his eyes. 'I'm the one who's loving it.'

He took his hands from her hips and cradled her in his arms, and she thought she sensed a change of mood in him. 'Really—loving it?' he asked.

Chas stood perfectly still for a long moment. Then she freed herself quietly. 'Are you afraid I'll be another Holly Maguire, Tom?'

'No, the opposite if anything,' he said rather abruptly. 'But before we go into that, there's something I need to tell you, Chas. Let's not let our soup get cold, though.'

It was homemade mushroom soup. The aroma alone was divine but Chas had difficulty finishing hers. She put her cup down, half empty, and picked up her glass. 'Do I need this?' she asked with an attempt at humour. 'You sounded rather serious.'

He grimaced, put his soup cup away from him and picked up his own glass. Then he stretched his long legs out and rubbed his chin with his knuckles. 'I'm thinking of leaving Cresswell after the wedding, and the honeymoon, naturally.'

Her lips parted. 'Why?'

'Oh, not for good, but there's a place I would rather be, there's a project I'd rather be working on for the time being.'

Chas swallowed but didn't say the word—Benindee.

'Would you—would you put in managers?' she asked. 'I get the feeling that without you there could be chaos.'

He smiled briefly. 'I've been thinking of offering Rupe the job for as long as he wants it.'

'Rupert!' Her eyes widened. 'What about his Olympic aspirations and so on? His parents and the ancestral halls?'

'You couldn't find a better place than Cresswell to prepare for that, although he'll need time off for events. All the same, Rupert is much more capable than many people give him credit for. And for a couple of years anyway, Vanessa would be on her home turf while their marriage settled down. I—I know Vanessa,' he said as he had once before, 'and I want her to have that chance.'

'That's lovely of you,' Chas responded warmly.

'I do have an ulterior motive.' He looked at her drily. 'It would free me up.'

Chas spoke before she stopped to think. 'To be honest, I think you need to get away. I sometimes sense a very real impatience and—frustration in you.' Then *she* stopped abruptly.

'Are you wondering where you and I come into all this?' he said.

Her throat worked. 'Is this place the cattle station Vanessa told me about? On Cape York?'

'Yes. When did she tell you that?'

'Only today. We were doing the seating plans in here.' She gestured to the framed photo on the mantelpiece. 'She showed me that. I had no idea at the time of—of any significance it might have for me.'

'There's no call for wedding consultants up there.'

He grimaced. 'On the other hand there are plenty of challenges. Not only do I propose to rescue the station but also to change direction away from cattle.'

Chas looked down at her glass then she frowned incredulously. 'Tom, you're not asking me to—to up sticks and go to Benindee with you?'

He shook his head and rubbed the bridge of his nose. 'I'm trying to explain why, if we do get further involved with each other, it might be a long-distance arrangement for a while. Of course I'd come back frequently—I'd have to, for other business affairs. You could come up frequently, and make your own assessment of the place.'

Chas thought swiftly. 'Did you know all this when, for example, you first kissed me?'

He said wearily, 'It's been at the back of my mind for years. But I couldn't see how I could leave my mother and Vanessa. Now I can, and, from what you overheard the other night, it's timely.'

'I can understand about Vanessa, but your mother?' she queried.

'Of course, she's always going to miss my father but the worst of it is over and, so long as Vanessa is happy and I'm happy, I think she will be too.' He paused. 'And to be honest, the way you were tonight pushed me another step closer—'

'You mean us?'

He half-smiled. 'Yes, but not only that. It led me to think you'd enjoy Benindee. As a matter of fact, that thought popped into my mind when you helped rescue young Adam. You possess the ingenuity and resourcefulness that goes well with station life.' He paused. 'And to be honest, the particular superficiality of bringing home a whole cocktail party for a barbecue, for example, is getting to me.'

'I was right,' Chas murmured. 'There's a side of you I don't know at all.'

He looked faintly amused. 'Not that I'm some kind of killjoy,' he gestured, 'or that I object to people having fun, but I think I need a bit more of a challenge in my life than I have at present.'

'Could it even be the lack of some kind of a rock in your life? Maybe a wife and children?' she suggested.

The look he cast was swift, very grey and impenetrable. 'You could be right.'

She rubbed her brow. 'I don't know what to say.'

'That's twice in one night.'

She looked at him helplessly.

'Life moves in mysterious ways sometimes.' He held out his hand to her.

She hesitated then put hers into it.

'What did you have in mind for our future, Chas?'

'All I had in mind at the moment...' she paused '...was not to let the rest of the world see that I was...different.'

He raised an eyebrow at her.

She pondered the wisdom of telling Tom Hocking he'd achieved something for her no other man had, and decided against it.

'Uh—I feel a little as if I don't know whether I'm on my head or my heels.' She smiled ruefully at him. 'Quite a lot—also to be honest.'

He was silent for a long moment then he raised her hand to his mouth and kissed it. 'Thank you. So, will we give it a go?'

Chas swallowed something in her throat. 'Could we wait until after the wedding? I really need to concentrate now, and we could add all sorts of complications to what is already—'

She broke off as he laughed and supplied, 'Already a whole can of worms?'

'You know what I mean.' She shook her head. 'This could be quite a coup, career-wise, for me.'

He sobered rather rapidly. 'Think we can? Wait?'

'It's only a few days, Tom.'

'Does that mean I'm not even allowed to kiss you for the next ten days?' he queried with that familiar, slightly arrogant tilt of his head.

'No—yes, in private, well…' Her tongue tripped over itself as she tried to think clearly. 'It's what it leads on to that's the problem.'

'Problem?'

She took a deep breath. 'You *know* what I mean, Tom Hocking!'

'I do,' he agreed lazily. 'All sorts of very private pleasure, wouldn't you say?'

Chas suffered a moment of very clear recall in an amazingly physical way. Her eyes widened, her breathing altered and her amazed reaction was: Surely he can't do this to me just with words!

She stood up abruptly.

He eyed her then got to his feet and reached for her.

'Tom,' she breathed, and stopped.

They stared at each other for a long, long moment. She took in the little lines beside his mouth, the way his hair flopped on his forehead; she breathed in the essence of him, pure man, flavoured with clean linen.

Then he cupped her face, and she shook from head to toe with desire and longing, but all he did was plant the lightest kiss on her lips, and let her go.

'Even a few days,' he said with patent irony, 'is going to be a hell of a long time.'

'Yes,' she whispered. 'On the other hand, afterwards, there'll be nothing to flaw it for us.'

His lips twisted. 'You're a hard person to argue with, Chas Bartlett. Very well, you've got your reprieve.' He turned away and picked up a sandwich.

Reprieve? Chas wondered. An odd choice of word, or particularly meant in a way she didn't understand?

Whatever, he went out of his way to be a pleasant companion while they ate their sandwiches and had another glass of champagne. He also told her a bit more about Benindee.

'It's in the Lakeland-Laura area, west and inland from Cooktown. It's a cattle station, but peanuts and coffee have really taken off in the area and that's what I plan to experiment with. Also sugar cane. It's beautiful country but, of course, hot.'

As Chas listened, she formed two impressions—it would be a frontier kind of life for a time, but it was also something he cared deeply about. She had a sudden vision of him in action mode on a far-flung property; decisive and effective as he brought it back to life. A vision of him testing himself physically against the elements and the country and, although it should have surprised her when she thought of the powerful, urbane businessman he could be, it didn't.

She'd always known, she reflected, that there was an action man in Tom Hocking. That was why it came as no surprise to discover that he could juggle boardrooms, high finance and the call of the wild. The thing to think about was—could she handle the call of the wild?

Then he took a phone call, and said rather abruptly, 'I'll call you back in a moment, Will.'

Chas took the hint. 'I'll go to bed. That sounded like business.'

'Yes, but—'

'Doesn't matter.' She smiled. 'It's been a big day and I'm starting to wilt.' She put her hand over his briefly. 'Goodnight.'

'Chas…'

But she took herself off with a wave.

Sleep didn't come easily.

What could be better, she asked herself, propped against her pillows in the dark, for someone like me? No mad rush to the altar, a leisurely, long-distance affair by the sound of it so I can get on with my life, my business and my career in between times—what's wrong with it?

I've made it plain enough I don't want to be rushed into anything but…

She paused in her thoughts and listened to the sounds of the barbecue. It was beginning to wind down at last, she guessed as she heard a car start up, and she resumed her reflections.

If I'd suggested it, it would have been OK—is that it? But that doesn't make sense. I'm not so bossy and stupid as to believe I can call all the shots. Normally, I'm the least bossy person I know. Tact and subtle persuasion are my fortes—or they used to be, she thought with irony.

She sat up suddenly. Even if I didn't agree to it, would I like to think he wanted to rush me to the altar as an assurance that he feels the same way I do? Is *that* it? But if it is, that's tantamount to saying *Here I go again*…it's everything to me, but maybe not so to him?

Why would I ever go through that again? she asked herself starkly.

Everything that could go wrong with a wedding started to go wrong the next day.

The flower-girl and page-boy, twins, were both diagnosed with chickenpox. The best man, Bill Edwards, still to arrive from the UK, rang to say he'd fallen off a horse—another horse-mad individual, Chas thought with gritted teeth—and broken his leg in a rather complicated way that precluded him flying to Australia in the near future.

The very stylish country inn, hired in total to house the overflow of the UK wedding contingent, closed its doors unexpectedly due to a marriage crisis between the couple who ran it.

The bride was heard to say, as the impact of all this sank in, that perhaps they were omens?

'Nonsense,' Tom said sharply at the urgent conference called. 'Between all our friends surely we can come up with another couple of kids roughly the same size? As for accommodation, surely we can make other arrangements? Chas?'

'Yes. I'll get on to that straight away.'

'Get on to Birdie too. She knows the area really well. Rupert, you're the only real problem, mate. Any ideas?'

'What about Robbie Whitelaw?' the earl suggested. Chas dropped her pen.

'Easier than getting someone from overseas at this late stage. He is family and we were rather sad that he wasn't going to be able to make the wedding, weren't we?'

How was he family? Chas wondered wildly.

The earl proceeded to explain that too. 'Robbie is married to our niece, my brother's daughter. He and Rupert became big chums, didn't you, Rupe?'

'Yes, we did.' Rupert frowned, however. 'But isn't he in Saudi Arabia doing something complicated with oil wells and couldn't get away for the wedding? Isn't that why Cousin Kate is coming on her own?'

'Not any more, darling,' Helen said. 'Kate rang me last night. They expect to arrive in Brisbane a couple of days before the wedding.' She turned to Vanessa. 'I was going to mention it so we could add him to the guest list. Oh, I think it would be a lovely idea!'

Chas stared down at her pad. Yes, Rob Whitelaw was called Robbie by a lot of his friends, although she had never done so.

Yes, she'd heard that Rob Whitelaw had married Katherine somebody or other and gone to live overseas. It had never entered her wildest calculations she'd be the niece of the Wickhams.

'Better yet,' Rupert smiled suddenly, 'Robbie and Bill are of a very similar build, if you're looking so horrified on that account, Chas. I'm sure Robbie could fit into Bill's suit!'

'Thank heavens for that,' she managed to murmur and wrote something quite illegible on her pad. 'Um…kids.' She looked up to see Tom watching her rather intently and made a supreme effort to go on smoothly, 'Should we make a list of likely replacements for the flower-girl and page-boy, poor poppets?'

It seemed she hadn't been smooth enough.

Tom waylaid her as she was about to drive into

Toowoomba to consult Birdie on guest houses. It was the first time they'd been alone since the previous day, a day and evening of amazing revelations.

She went into her bedroom to get her car keys.

He followed her in, coming from the opposite direction, and closed the door. 'What's up?'

'What do you mean?'

'Do you happen to know Robbie Whitelaw?'

She gasped. 'How did you guess?'

'You went quite pale.'

Chas's shoulders sagged. 'He's my ex-fiancé. I can't believe this could happen to me.'

'Would you like me to have him taken out at dawn and shot?'

She smiled faintly. 'Yes, please. No, of course not!'

'I could have a word with Rupert,' he suggested.

'No. We can't stop him from coming to the wedding as a guest anyway. No! I'll be fine. It just came out of the blue at me and I guess on top of chickenpox, inn closures and the like, it was enough to make any wedding consultant go a bit pale.'

He grinned then sobered almost immediately. 'Sure?'

'Sure.'

He didn't answer immediately but searched her eyes thoroughly. Then he said thoughtfully, 'I could provide some back-up.'

She looked a question at him.

'Say we brushed aside this veil of secrecy—I don't think there's much point to it, personally—you would have something with which to counter Lady Katherine Whitelaw. Not that I'm aristocracy but—'

'She's a lady in her own right?' Chas said a little blankly. 'I suppose she would be.'

'You didn't know that.' It was a statement, not a question.

'No. Not that it makes any difference.'

'Precisely. So. What do you think?'

Chas stared up at him. 'Tom, no and thank you, but I'd rather wait until after the wedding.'

He paused and watched her narrowly. 'Is it Benindee?'

She blinked several times. 'How do you mean?'

'Chas,' he said deliberately, 'your ban on any kind of relations between us after what happened yesterday is based on entirely superfluous objections. My mother won't mind—she's actually delighted, from some of the little hints she's dropped. My sister won't mind—'

'Your mother can't have any idea!'

'I don't know how the hell she worked it out but she has,' he said flatly. 'Vanessa won't mind—she really likes you—so…your reservations have got to do either with Benindee—or Robbie Whitelaw.'

'It's…it's only a few days to—to the wedding,' she stammered.

'It may be, but it's now or never for us. Are we an item, Miss Bartlett, or are we not?'

She'd never seen his grey eyes so hard, she'd never seen that tilt of his head so arrogant.

She started to speak several times but couldn't make any sense, then the words came from somewhere. 'If you're expecting me to jump into bed with you, Tom—'

'I can guarantee you'd love it.'

Her nostrils pinched. 'Jump into bed with you right *now*, you mistake me—'

'Not right now, naturally,' he broke in. 'We could even leave that until after the wedding—your golden age for us,' he said satirically, 'but I want to know where we stand. Right *now*,' he mimicked angrily.

'Then I'll tell you. It's not Benindee, it's you. No, we're not an item, Tom, and would you please go away before I throw things? How you expect me to cope with your mad family on top of…' She trailed off.

'Or,' he suggested softly, 'are you leaving your options open, Chas? Until you meet up with your ex-fiancé again, for example?'

She drew a shaky breath, incredulous that he could believe this of her. 'How can you—?'

'If that's the case—' he overrode her autocratically '—let's set a benchmark of what's between us for you to measure him up to.'

'Set a…?' Her eyes were huge.

'Like this,' he drawled, and pulled her into his arms.

Chas opened her mouth.

'Don't say a word,' he cautioned, 'until I've done this. We could call it a scientific experiment if you like.'

'Tom…'

He trailed his fingers down the back of her neck then up again and gently tugged her hair. Her face lifted to his. He kissed her briefly then he moved his hand down from her head to spread his fingers over the small of her back. With his other hand he flicked open the two top buttons of her cream cotton shirt, and proceeded to caress the swell of her breasts above her bra.

She sucked in a breath and said huskily, 'You may think you have the right to kiss me however and whenever you like but—'

'Wait a moment,' he said barely audibly, his fingers

on one nipple beneath the flimsy silk of her bra, then the other. 'Ah, I thought they might do that,' he murmured, as they peaked. 'You were saying?'

A tremor ran down her body and she looked into his eyes helplessly as she felt his body stir against her own. Not only that, but every inch of him, all the sleek muscles, the hard wall of his chest, the compact hips and long legs also excited her almost unbearably. Even the faint smell of horses coming from his bush shirt and jeans, those riveting grey eyes, the lines and angles of his face—all of it spoke to her like the intensely masculine equivalent of a siren song.

'Did he ever do this to you?' he queried, dispassionately observing all the signs of her arousal.

Chas drew a shaken, broken breath then she felt a surge of anger coursing through her veins and discovered she could no longer dam up the truth, from herself or him.

'N-no,' she said unevenly, 'but you could say I'm running scared of being an ''item'' with you. Scared of your scientific experiments and a long-distance affair where we each live our own lives and only come together for sex. Yes, you could say that, Tom.'

His eyes bored into hers. 'You forgot to mention it was marriage you were after, Chas. In fact you've done nothing to correct the impression you gave me that you were not into serious relationships at all.'

'That's not what I'm after. I'm after the part of you that would mean so much to me, I couldn't live without it. But I haven't yet found that because I don't think you want to surrender it. It's the part of me that should matter more to *you* than anything. That's what's missing between us, Tom.'

'And those are the things that generally come along the way,' he countered swiftly.

'They may do. For others. I need to know they're in place before I make another ghastly mistake. I'm sorry.' Tears pooled in her eyes but she brushed them away. 'I'm truly sorry.' She turned away.

She heard the bedroom door open and close a moment later.

She put her hands to her face and couldn't prevent the tears from trickling between her fingers but, although she hadn't been able to put a name to her deepest fears last night, she knew she'd got it right today.

She didn't want to be anyone's long-distance mistress, but to be Tom's would hurt unbearably. She did believe there was a part of him she might never uncover.

He'd also been right when he'd sensed she was looking for a reprieve—the word she'd wondered about last night. Had that, in part, accounted for his actions today?

But even if that meant they knew each other rather well, was it well enough?

'No,' she murmured and licked some salty tears from her top lip.

And better, she thought, for it to have happened now. Not that anything could feel less painful to her at the moment, but it would have to hurt more the longer it lasted.

A treacherous thought slid through her mind. Would she have been happy to abandon her career and go and live on a cattle station she'd never seen, if she'd been asked to?

I suppose I can't take Benindee out of the equation completely, she conceded, but it was all so sudden!

And how was she going to survive the next few days?

CHAPTER NINE

'Tom's gone away on business again,' Vanessa said worriedly when Chas got back from Toowoomba and her session with Birdie. 'I wish he wouldn't do this!'

'Darling,' Harriet consoled her, 'you can't expect him to stand still because of a wedding. Where's he gone this time?' she asked, somewhat negating her efforts at consolation.

'Melbourne. That's all he said—he left the message with Arnold. And I hadn't even got around to pinning him down to try on his suit!'

'Ahem,' Arnold said from behind them. 'I forgot to mention that bit of his message. The suit fits, he said to tell you.'

'There you go!' Clare beamed around. 'All sorted.'

But Vanessa still looked disconsolate. 'I just feel more comfortable with Tom around.'

Chas decided it was time to intervene—she'd been unable to decide whether she felt deep relief or deep regret at Tom's departure. 'You've still got me. I know I don't measure up to Tom,' she said humorously, 'but I have managed to find another guest house to take the overflow. It's very nice; a little bit further away but just as nice, in fact, as the first one.'

'Bravo, Chas!' Harriet clapped her hands. 'So it's only the kids we need to sort out. Would you believe that amongst our many friends there is not one pair of same-size children available for the wedding? They're all either too small or too big.'

Chas ruminated for a moment. The flower-girl dress and page-boy outfit were finished, she'd actually brought them up with her, confident that there wouldn't be any last-minute adjustments to be made. Just goes to show, she thought.

'OK. Is there a sewing machine up here?' she queried.

'Of course,' Harriet responded. 'Not that *we* actually use it but we have a sewing lady who comes in once a month.'

'Fine. Is there, amongst the smaller brigade, any kids that particularly appeal to you, Vanessa?'

'Well,' Vanessa thought for a moment, 'there's Lottie and Brad Kincaid. Brad is a year younger than Martin and Lottie's, what, six? That makes her two years younger than Miranda. But they're rather sweet kids and their mum's one of my best friends.'

'Get them for me,' Chas said succinctly. 'I might be able to downsize the outfits rather than go through the rigmarole of getting new ones made at this late stage.'

'Is there anything you can't do, Chas?' Vanessa enquired, looking brighter.

Yes: please your brother, Chas thought with a pang of pain but did not say.

Tom stayed away on business for two days.

During that time the final fittings and the test run of hair and make-up went off smoothly and Chas managed to alter the page-boy and flower-girl outfits successfully.

It also rained for a couple of days then cleared up brilliantly.

'Should be fine now we've got that out of our system,' Clare remarked.

The Wickhams and Rupert went away again for a few days, then it was only four days to go and the overseas guests started to arrive. Chas made herself as scarce as she could but it wasn't only Vanessa and Harriet who breathed sighs of relief when Tom came home as the crowd of wedding guests grew, Chas did too, in spite of her turmoil of emotions.

She met him at dinner, although not as a guest.

There were fourteen for dinner, not a problem for the table, which extended to sixteen places. Not a problem with china, silverware or glassware, there was an abundance of that.

Nervous tension in the kitchen was another matter, so Chas took Harriet aside that morning and suggested that if Arnold could be allowed to concentrate on his cooking while she supervised the rest of it, they might avoid any trauma. Harriet agreed with a sigh of relief.

So Chas and Arnold worked side by side all afternoon.

She set the table, she made the canapés for the pre-dinner drinks, she assisted with all the dishes Arnold was preparing and took charge of the cheese and fruit boards to be served before dessert, and nominated herself to provide the coffee and liqueurs after dessert.

At five o'clock she took a bit of a break but she was back on board by six o'clock, dressed in a plain chocolate linen dress and a comfortable pair of matching suede shoes with little heels.

'You still look as if you should be going to this dinner, not serving it,' Arnold remarked when she reappeared in his kitchen.

'No way! Too dressy? I thought I looked rather housekeeperly.'

'I don't think you ever could,' Arnold said candidly, 'but anyway, we can relax a bit; Tom's home.'

Tom's home, Chas thought. That says so much! All the same, while I'm thinking, *Thank heavens! He can take charge*—I'm suddenly a nervous wreck.

'Surely this is a bit above and beyond the call of duty, Aphrodite?' Tom Hocking said *sotto voce* as Chas served his first course of prosciutto, melon, olives and mayonnaise.

Their gazes clashed until she looked away down the length of the table with its thirteen other guests.

'Not at all, sir,' she murmured, and withdrew.

The next course was grilled fillets of fish served in a parsley sauce. Tom allowed it to be served and his plate retrieved without comment.

'How have you been in my absence, Miss Bartlett? Still hell-bent on running scared?' he asked as she placed roast duckling garnished with maraschino cherries in front of him and offered him a platter of vegetables to choose from.

'I've been exceedingly well, thank you. Would you care for any of these or all of them or would you prefer to have them in your lap?'

He smiled with tigerish amusement. 'Now how would that look on a wedding consultant's résumé— *Got fired at the last minute on account of causing grievous bodily harm to the bride's brother*? I'll have a bit of all of them, thank you. By the way, you have a strand of hair caught against your lipstick.' He brushed it aside with his forefinger.

Chas gritted her teeth and made no reply.

Finally, the dinner, which had gone swimmingly, got to the coffee stage.

It was such a beautiful night, Chas decided to put it all outside on the veranda and to let everyone help themselves—and there was no more for her to do. There were two extra kitchen hands, one of them Mary Baxter, to do the clearing up.

There was no way the tension she was suffering would allow her to sleep either so she changed into shorts and T-shirt, put on her jogging shoes and went for a run. She went out by the back door and whistled for Leroy and Piccanin. They came immediately, enchanted at the idea.

She jogged down towards the stallion barn and on towards the main gates. She was halfway there when she overtook a small figure trudging along with a suitcase. It turned out to be Adam Baxter.

'Adam!' She stopped next to him. 'What on earth are you doing? Shouldn't you be in bed?'

'Yes, but I'm running away.'

'Running…?' Chas paused. 'Why?'

'Nobody loves me.' He shrugged. 'Nobody understands me. All they ever do is shout at me!'

'What have you done now?' Chas enquired, hiding a smile.

'It wasn't my fault,' Adam said passionately. 'I was only trying to help. How was I to know Mum would hate the idea?'

'You'd better start at the beginning.'

'Well, she was going on about how we might not be able to afford a holiday this year because she needs a new car. So I got this tin and I stuck a sign on it—''The Baxter Family Holiday Fund''—and every afternoon for a week I collected money in town while I was waiting for the bus home from school.'

'Oh, dear.' Chas had trouble controlling her voice. 'Did you do any good?'

'Yep. I was up to about fifty dollars then a policeman stopped me and reported me to Mum.'

'And she was a bit mad?'

'A bit mad? Anyone would think I'd robbed a bank! And they made me donate it all to charity!'

'And Brendan didn't know what you were doing?'

'No, he gets a later bus.'

'I see,' Chas said. 'Well, Adam, the thing is, I do admire your entrepreneurial spirit but I can't let you run away. Let's go home before your poor mum finds out. Besides which, I've just had a thought. Maybe Tom could give you a job so you could earn a bit of money legitimately.'

'Like what?'

'Washing cars—never, ever driving them, though, uh…maybe that's not such a good idea. Uh…'

She stopped as a glow lit up the drive and shortly thereafter they were illuminated by a pair of powerful headlights.

'That's Tom,' Adam said, just a shade nervously.

It was Tom, not in a good mood. He got out of his car and surveyed them for a moment then said curtly to Chas, 'Are you helping him to run away or hindering him?'

'What do you think?' she tossed back at him.

'What I *know* is that his mother's frantic, and so is Brendan. Hop in, Adam, and don't ever pull this stunt again.'

'No, sir,' Adam mumbled and hopped into the car with his suitcase.

'So what *are* you doing out here, Chas?'

'Taking a run! If you don't believe me, ask Leroy

and Piccanin. What on earth do you imagine I'm doing?'

'I have no idea. Your thought processes are a mystery to me. Ask Leroy and Piccanin?'

'Just go away, Tom,' she advised wearily then she remembered Adam. 'No, hang on a moment. Could you find a job for Adam? I think he needs it.'

'He's only ten.'

'It might keep him out of mischief as well as provide some pocket money. Some…some gardening or something like that.'

'Why don't you suggest it to my mother? She'd love the idea of letting Adam loose in her beloved gardens.'

Chas glared at him but he simply got back into the car and she heard him say to Adam, more gently, 'Listen, mate, we've got some new rules. If you've got any problems or any ideas, bring them to me first and we'll have a chat. Deal?'

'Deal,' Adam replied fervently.

Chas turned away as they drove off and continued her jog.

When she got back to her bedroom she was nicely tired and she fell asleep with no trouble. In the middle of the night she woke up and burst into tears.

How could she be in such discord with a man she…she what? she wondered as the painful sobs racked her.

A man who'd go out searching for a runaway child late at night and take time to help him too in a way that had really touched her.

Someone, despite his earlier barbs, whose hard, shuttered expression on the driveway had reached her for a few seconds in a curious way, a way that she could now identify as a longing to share his burdens.

A man without whom, when he wasn't around, she felt just as bereft as his sister did.

A man who, despite being hard to read, touched her emotionally to her very depths? A man she wanted to know through and through because there was so much she valued about him even when she didn't know him through and through. Did that make sense? Especially after some of the things he'd said tonight?

It didn't have to, she answered herself. It had happened whether she liked it or not. Yet she was running scared. Well, perhaps she had reason to but was it unreasonable to at least find out what came along the way for them?

It was also true that she *had* told him she wasn't into serious relationships, and had done nothing to correct that impression—the opposite, if anything!

Had it been unreasonable to impose restrictions on them until after the wedding?

If only it wasn't for this damn wedding, she thought and buried her face in her hands. I can't think straight. But—is it only me being unreasonable?

She slept in the next morning but was pleased to find that made her the last person to go to breakfast, on her own.

At least she thought she'd be on her own, but just as she was pouring her coffee Tom came in.

'Morning, Chas,' he said briskly.

'Good morning,' she murmured.

He grinned. 'I saw you looking like this once before. When we bumped into each other on the Gold Coast.'

'Yes, well, we may not be each other's favourite person any more now than we were then.'

He poured his own coffee and sat down opposite her. 'Like me to go away again?'

'No,' she said hastily.

He raised a wry eyebrow at her.

'You do represent the ultimate authority around here,' she explained. 'And do we ever need that.' She looked down and stirred some sugar into her coffee.

'Actually, Chas, without you, we would never have got this far. I do appreciate the way you've bucked in.'

'Thank you,' she said tonelessly and sipped her coffee. It was too hot and she winced as she burnt her lip.

'Nor…' He paused and studied her lazily. 'Nor am I insensitive enough not to see that our personal differences are making it harder for you.'

'What am I supposed to say to that?' she queried huskily.

'Whatever you like. "Go to hell, Tom Hocking," or, "That's very thoughtful of you, Tom!" What about…?' He ruminated for a moment, looking satirical. 'Yes, how about, "I don't give a damn!" Short, sweet and to the point.'

'If you're quite finished—'

'Not by a country mile, as the saying goes. Your ex is due to arrive this afternoon.'

'I know.' She tried her coffee again.

'How do you propose to handle it?'

She frowned. 'What do you suggest? I'm certainly not going to introduce myself to his wife as the girl he almost married.'

'I didn't think you would but—good. She's pregnant, you see.'

Chas caught her breath and Tom Hocking watched her narrowly with no sign of amusement, satirical or otherwise.

'I thought it might help to be forewarned,' he said then, rather gently.

'I… Thank you, but—I hope they're very happy.'

'If you mean that, Chas, what are we really fighting about?'

She closed her eyes. 'I tried to explain.'

'And I got on my high horse and rode off into the sunset, speaking metaphorically.' His lips twisted. 'Would you at least come and see Benindee with me one day, after the wedding is over, naturally?'

'I thought…I thought the way you were last night and—'

'Men and their egos don't part easily, Chas.'

'Yes, I would like to,' she said barely audibly.

'Good.' He turned his head at approaching voices. 'The mob,' he said wryly. 'By the way, Adam Baxter is now on the payroll.'

Chas sat up enthusiastically. 'That's wonderful! What did you find for him to do?'

'Something with the least destructive potential I could come up with. He's now the official dog keeper. He has to brush Leroy and Piccanin, check them for ticks, clean out their kennels daily and bath them once a week. He also expressed the desire to teach them a few tricks.'

Chas's expression changed to one of comic apprehension. 'The least destructive potential? The mind boggles at the thought of Adam and Leroy in cahoots!'

He laughed. 'It was all I could come up with. At least it might keep him from begging on the streets. Ah, the bride-and groom-to-be,' he said as Vanessa and Rupert came in. 'How's it going, guys?'

'Well, it's good to see you in a good mood again,' Vanessa enthused and put her arm affectionately around her brother. 'I thought you were in a paddy about something.'

'Me? What gave you that idea?'

'I have known you all my life, Tom.'

'Well, I'm not any longer,' he assured her. 'In fact I'm entirely at your disposal, sister mine. Just tell me what you want me to do.' He got up and the three of them left the dining room laughing.

Chas sat on for a few minutes while she finished her coffee and examined a strange thought—she had discovered that Tom and Vanessa were much closer than they appeared on the surface. So—to what lengths would Tom Hocking go to ensure his sister's happiness, or at least a smooth path to her wedding?

Was that a nasty suspicion to cherish or a natural reaction on the part of someone still stinging from the lash of his tongue during their two previous encounters despite her revelations of the night?

I don't know, she decided. I can only play it by ear.

'Well,' Katherine Whitelaw, six months pregnant, said that afternoon, 'so you're the genius my aunt's been telling me about? The last word in wedding consultants. How do you do?' She shook Chas's hand and turned to the man beside her. 'This is my husband, Robbie.'

'I did wonder if it was the same Rob Whitelaw—hello, Rob!' Chas said. 'How are you?'

Robbie Whitelaw was lost for words but he recovered swiftly. 'Chas! What a small world.' He was fair, rugged and good-looking.

'You're not wrong!' Chas said and waited for some reaction within her to the man she'd so nearly married. Nothing came other than a sense of disbelief that all

Rob seemed to mean to her now was a distant life she might as well have lived on another planet...

'You two know each other?' Katherine queried. She was pretty with a short cap of dark hair and a heart-shaped face. Was she the woman in Rob's past, though, or someone he had been able to convince he could bury the past for her? Was there a slightly petulant, suspicious look in her dark eyes?

'Yes, in Brisbane, a few years ago, we did,' she replied casually.

'So you're still in the wedding business, Chas?'

'As you see! And I gather you're still an engineer. I think Rupert might have been right. You look as if the best-man suit will fit you to a T, which is a great relief to me,' she said with a humorous look. 'And just to fill you both in, we're having the church rehearsal this evening.'

'Yes.' Tom came up and introduced himself. 'Welcome to Cresswell. Chas, your mother's on the phone—in my study. I'll be with you in a moment.' He ushered the Whitelaws towards Harriet and came back immediately to where Chas was standing transfixed.

'Something's wrong, isn't it?' she said hoarsely.

He took her hand and led her out of earshot of the others. 'Your father's had a stroke, Chas. They think it's only a mild one at this stage but I can fly you down to Brisbane right now.'

'That was so kind of you,' Chas said when Tom landed her at Archerfield Airport in a light plane and had a hire car waiting for her.

'On the contrary, it was the least I could do after all you've done for us. Got that list?'

On the flight he'd suggested, if she could think straight, that she compose a list of all the things he needed to attend to in her place.

She handed it to him. 'I'll be back as soon as I can,' she promised.

He took her hand. 'You stay as long as you're needed, although…' he smiled into her eyes '…if you could stand by your mobile, that would be a big help, no doubt.'

'I will. I will!'

'Off you go, then.' He bent his head and kissed her briefly. 'Let me know how he is, and also if there's anything I can do.'

'Oh, Chas, I knew he should slow down.' Hope Bartlett wept into her daughter's shoulder. 'And now I've had to drag you away from your wonderful wedding, but—'

'Shh…' Chas stroked her mother's hair. 'The only important thing is Dad.'

Vanessa's wedding day dawned bright and clear.

A helicopter, not piloted by Tom this time, picked Chas up at Archerfield and flew her directly to Cresswell early in the morning.

Both Harriet and Vanessa were on hand to greet Chas. 'How is he? Your father?' Harriet asked immediately.

'He's going to be fine. There's no loss of speech and minimal paralysis, which they hope to reverse, but he's going to have to re-evaluate his lifestyle and that isn't going to be easy for him. For example—' she smiled '—when he realised I was at his bedside rather than up here on the eve of your wedding, Vanessa, he nearly had a fit!'

Vanessa hugged her. 'Oh, thank you for coming back and I intend to thank your father one day, too! I love you, Chas!'

'How's it going?' Chas asked Harriet, when they were on their own.

'My dear, Tom has been simply wonderful! But it's not quite the same without you.'

'Then I'd better get stuck in!'

She was everywhere, checking out the marquee, supervising the placement of the tables and chairs, the decorations and the flowers, the caterers.

She bumped into Tom several times. He was the only male member of the wedding party left on Cresswell; Rupert, the best man and the ushers had been removed along with the Wickhams to the guest house.

Tom offered her his services in any way she needed them. She directed him to be in charge of the setting up of the bar.

She organised a light lunch and took some informal photos of the bride, her mother and aunt, her bridesmaids, flower-girl and page-boy, as well as Tom, all hamming it up.

Then it was time to get serious about Vanessa's four o'clock appointment at the church.

While everyone was getting dressed Chas changed too, lightning-fast, into a beige silk suit that was elegant but discreet.

When everyone was ready she cracked open some bottles of champagne, and as the glasses were handed around she said, 'I'd like to propose a toast.' She raised her glass. 'To Vanessa, a simply exquisite bride. May you and Rupert have a long and happy life together. And to everyone else—you all look gorgeous too!'

A happy hubbub broke out.

'That was inspired,' Tom said quietly to her. He'd almost taken her breath away in his morning suit.

'I've found it usually works, settles a few butterflies and so on. And—' she consulted her watch '—we're actually running on time!'

'You know, the army could use you.'

'But could I use the army?' she replied with a faint smile. 'Ready, Mr Hocking? Your sister awaits you.'

'When I've done this.' He raised his glass. 'Another toast is in order, I think you'll all agree. To Chas— what would we have done without her?' He put his glass down, put his arms around her and kissed her. 'Thank you for everything.' There was a delighted chorus of applause.

The rest of the day and evening slipped by.

There were no major glitches. The service went smoothly and was beautiful. The emotion between Tom and Vanessa was tangible as he gave her away. Vanessa was radiant, Rupert was inspired and Loretta Quinn's harp music was triumphal as they made their way down the aisle.

Everyone who worked on the stud made a presentation to Vanessa and Rupert while the photos were being taken, of a bronze horse and rider Chas had found for them in an antiques shop.

The journey down the drive in a carriage and pair for the couple went smoothly. The meal was fine; the troupe of jugglers had to do two encores and then only got away with difficulty. The speeches went without a hitch, and then everyone settled down to some serious partying and dancing.

That was when Chas looked around the flower-filled, candlelit marquee at the happy guests, the happy couple, and blew out her cheeks in a *phew!* of relief as she decided she could relax for a bit.

'My sentiments entirely.' Tom loomed up beside her and took her elbow. 'Make that a double phew!'

She had to laugh.

'Come and sit down. I don't suppose you thought to eat, or drink?'

'I did snatch a bite earlier but no, I've certainly not drunk as in alcohol and perhaps I'd better not. It might send me to sleep.'

'Yes, you better had,' he disagreed, and led her to a table and procured a glass of wine for her. 'One glass can't do any harm.'

'There's still the cutting of the cake, the going away—'

'Chas, don't argue,' he advised and looked into her eyes. 'I'm not about to take no for an answer.'

'Just as you feel entirely entitled to kiss me whenever the whim takes you,' she grumbled, then took a sip of wine. 'You're right, that's nice.'

'Yes, I do. Kissing each other seems to come naturally to us, though.'

'I feel sure I should be able to find a flaw in that but I haven't got the energy.'

He grinned. 'That's a relief. Do you dance?'

'Not at my weddings.'

'Let's make an exception to that rule. For one thing—' he rubbed his knuckles along his jaw '—if you don't see yourself as part of the family by now, we do.'

Chas sipped some more wine and smiled a little dreamily. 'That's really nice of you, Tom, but—'

'Oh, have a little dance with him, please!' Vanessa leant over her shoulder and smiled impishly. 'We're all going insane wondering what's between you two and how we can promote it!' She waltzed away.

'See?' Tom raised his eyebrow at Chas.

He'd discarded the jacket of his morning suit but still wore the pearl-grey waistcoat over his shirt. Beneath his shirt cuffs there was some dark springy hair on his wrists and it had the most curious effect on Chas.

She suddenly visualised him in the pool in the creek, sleek and nearly naked; strong and beautiful and above all able to bring her the wild rapture she hadn't known and could never forget.

He got up carefully, as if he was fully aware he'd aroused some memories for her and didn't want to break the spell. He put his hand out; she hesitated, then put hers into it and got to her feet.

'Take it easy,' he murmured as she stumbled once. 'I know it doesn't come naturally but let me do the work.'

She smiled ruefully up at him and did as commanded. It became blissful. He held her lightly but gave her expert direction. She was surprised at first at what a good dancer he was, then she thought of his excellent co-ordination and wondered why she'd assumed a lack of rhythm in him.

If anyone suffered a lack of rhythm, she was the one. She blamed it on her poor sense of direction and often found dancing a trial unless she was allowed to do her own thing, but with Tom it was different.

'Well, well,' he said softly. 'Could this be the one area where I can lead and you can follow?'

It was on the tip of her tongue to say, *No, there's another very specific area that falls into that category*—but she blushed instead.

'What now, Aphrodite?' he queried.

'Nothing. Not anything I can tell you about here, anyway.'

His eyebrows shot up. 'Do you have any idea what that does to me?'

A laugh trembled on her lips then she sobered. 'Were you serious about showing me Benindee?'

He frowned. 'Of course. Why would you think otherwise?'

'In a very small-minded moment,' she confessed, 'I did wonder if you were simply pulling out all the stops to get this wedding accomplished smoothly.'

His hand on her back moved and he stroked her neck with his fingers. 'That was small-minded.'

'You had, only the day before, said some rather unpleasant things to me,' she pointed out.

'I remember them well.' He chewed his lip. 'I was even rather proud of them at the time, bastard that I can be but, no, Benindee was a peace offering. We could go tomorrow.'

She stirred in his arms. 'I need some time with my father, Tom.'

'Of course, sorry. I forgot. When he's well enough, then?'

'With pleasure.'

They said no more for a while. The music was slow and dreamy; all that was really required was to sway to it in each other's arms. Then the band got lively and Tom danced her out of the marquee onto the lawn.

'I—' She started to say.

'I know you take your responsibilities very seriously,

dear wedding consultant,' he cut in softly, 'but it's a choice of being kissed in public—or private.' He stopped as a man about to go back into the marquee bumped into them.

It was Rob Whitelaw.

'Well, well,' he drawled, 'if it isn't the bride's brother and my ex-fiancée!'

Chas froze and she felt Tom stiffen.

'So?' he said to Rob Whitelaw.

'Nothing.' Rob gestured. 'I hope you find her easier to satisfy than I did, that's all.'

Chas felt the sudden bunching of Tom's muscles beneath her hands and she clutched him urgently. 'No, no, *please*,' she breathed, 'no violence. Please, Tom!'

Rob Whitelaw walked into the tent.

Chas turned away and was physically sick.

CHAPTER TEN

HALF an hour later she was alone in Tom's study, where he'd led her after she'd freshened up in her bedroom.

'Stay there,' he'd commanded. 'I'll get some coffee sent in and I'll let my mother know you're off-duty now.'

It said something for Chas's state of mind that she hadn't raised a protest.

She was drinking Arnold's coffee when Tom came back.

'How's it going?' she asked.

'Fine. We have an hour before they change and go away. I told them it had all been a bit much for you on top of your father's stroke. They understand and they send their love.' He closed the door and came to sit down opposite her. 'You should have let me flatten the bastard,' he added.

Chas closed her eyes.

'Listen,' Tom said after a moment during which he'd studied her narrowly, 'you need to talk about it, not bury it away.'

'Talk about what?' Chas lifted her eyes to his, and they were tear-filled. 'How could I have been so taken in, such a fool and—?'

'I'd say he's good at that. He's obviously taken Rupert in, the earl, the countess—'

'But that's different,' Chas said intensely. 'That's so

different from getting within a whisker of marrying a man I didn't read at all.' She shook her head.

Tom reached for his coffee. 'He may have taken everyone in initially, but his wife could be a different matter now. There's something about Katherine Whitelaw that suggests discontent. She was quite snappy with him during the dinner. If they're not happy, he may be regretting you and making nasty remarks in consequence. What did he mean?'

She shivered.

'Chas—'

'Tom,' she interrupted, 'when I first saw Rob again it was as if we'd existed on another planet, in another life. I thought—I'm free at last of all the memories, all the wrong readings I took, all the miscalculations I made about him, and myself.'

'But in one brutal sentence he demolished that freedom?' he hazarded. 'Chas, don't be a fool. Don't let a few words wreck it. Do you think I haven't made my own miscalculations, taken some wrong readings? I told you about Holly. Do you think many of us sail through life unscathed in that regard? What did he mean?' he added again.

She put her cup down and plaited her fingers, unable to frame the words.

'That you'd let him down by not understanding his predicament?' he suggested after a long moment.

'He did seem to think that because I was head over heels in love with him, I should be satisfied by his assurances it wouldn't come between us.'

Tom smiled. 'That sounds like men and their egos again.'

'That's what I thought.' Chas sniffed and dashed at

her eyes. 'Or, he could have been referring to the fact that I wasn't very good in bed.'

Tom stared at her. 'Is that what *you* thought?' he queried with an incredulous frown. 'Or would that have been something he planted in your mind?'

'I don't know. I was a virgin. I certainly felt very attracted to him.' She swallowed. 'But the fact of the matter was I never quite made…it, although sometimes I used to fake it. I used to…to tell myself it was probably a romantic myth…' She stopped awkwardly.

'Instantaneous cataclysmic comings of the earth-shaking variety for everyone? It probably is a romantic myth,' he said matter-of-factly, then grinned. 'Instantaneous cataclysmic comings—ICCs.'

Chas blinked. 'Is that a common acronym?'

'No.' He laughed softly. 'Just came to mind. Might be easier for you to handle, actually.' He sobered. 'But you couldn't quite convince yourself you were not abnormal in some way? Or,' he looked at her, 'convince yourself that it takes two to tango?'

She heaved a great sigh. 'I— Exactly. I kept telling myself it would come in time and worrying about it was probably the worst thing I could do but…' She opened her hands.

'Did it seem to matter to him?'

'Not really,' she said slowly. 'So long as he was…' She couldn't go on.

'So long as he was OK it was all OK?' he suggested. She nodded after a moment.

'Chas,' he put the cup down, 'you did the right thing. I'd like to bet that Robbie Whitelaw has one priority: himself.'

'That's all very well,' Chas said carefully, 'but—'

'You can't let go of your inferiority complex? Why

would you let him do that to you? How could it be more powerful than what *we* do to each other? May I point out that we don't even know each other in the exact biblical sense but we are, in fact, ICC in-place already.'

She had to smile, then she looked away and blushed.

He sat back. 'Is that what you were thinking about earlier before all this blew up? While we were dancing?'

'Yes,' she admitted.

'So?'

She stared at him with her throat working and the strangest feeling gripping her—as if her life to date had been an unfinished jigsaw puzzle with the last pieces only falling into place now...

'I've just realised I've been living in a time warp,' she said dazedly. 'I couldn't let go of my own wedding, my own failure, so I went out of my way to live everyone else's.'

'Then throw it all up and come to Benindee with me, Chas.'

She stared at him. 'I couldn't just— It would take me a few months to wind it all down.'

'That's fine with me.' She thought he watched her rather carefully for a moment. Then he shrugged. 'It'll take me a couple of months to put a bit more comfort in on the place, and hand over to Rupert here.'

'What—what would I do up there, though?'

'Do? What you're superb at. Organisation. The homestead—anything that takes your fancy. Stock, pasture control, water conservation, noxious weeds, coffee cultivation, peanut stooks—'

'Stop.' She held up her hand but she was laughing. 'You're not serious?'

'I am.' He grinned but then he did look serious. 'It's also an area rich in Aboriginal history and rock art. Then there's Benindee itself. There's an old proverb— *A mountain and a river make good neighbours.* We've got them both.'

She opened her mouth, closed it, then she said, 'Do you really want me to do this, Tom? Come and live with you?'

'Chas,' he said slowly, 'I think it has to be all or nothing for us now. Either we're together or we—part.' His gaze was steady and powerfully compelling.

She took an uncertain breath. There could be no doubt that even if it made sense, it was also an ultimatum he was issuing. Or a request for commitment? she wondered. Perhaps both. How would she ever know unless she put herself on the line too?

'All right. I was getting tired of weddings anyway before I fully understood. So. How?'

He gave it some thought. 'Let's make a date. I fly you up to Benindee in—three months' time?'

'That's…that's all?' Her eyes were wide.

'Yes.' His smile was curiously twisted this time. 'That way there can be no undue pressures on either of us, no—associations of the past to get in the way. Not,' he added, 'that I'm saying it's going to be easy.'

'No.' She trembled suddenly as she looked at him. 'We will talk to each other, though, won't we?'

'Of course. We'll see each other as well. I'll no doubt be backwards and forwards often. I'm sure,' he said softly, 'we'll be able to reignite the things we do to each other.'

'You could be right.' She gazed at him. 'I feel much better already,' she confessed.

'Good.' He sat forward and took her hand. 'One

thing, though, do you want to at least see Benindee before you go ahead and dismantle your business?'

She paused and concentrated on the steady pressure of his fingers on hers. Then she looked into his eyes. 'Tom, whatever had happened, I would be dismantling it. It's over for me now. I really need to move on.'

'Sure?'

'Quite sure. However, before they go away, could you bring Rupert and Vanessa in to say goodbye? I wouldn't feel right if I didn't see them—not only from a business point of view but also because they're friends now.'

'Of course.' He glanced at his watch. 'Should be round about that time, anyway. Stay here, I'll get them.' He got up, planted a kiss on her forehead then strode out.

'Oh, Chas.' Vanessa threw her arms around Chas. She looked stunning in her scarlet going-away outfit. 'Thank you so much for everything. You made it a simply perfect day and—I brought you this.'

It was a single cream rosebud from her bouquet.

Chas hugged her back. 'Thank you,' she murmured out of a clogged throat. 'I'll press it and keep it always. Have a lovely honeymoon.' She disengaged and turned to Rupert, then she hugged him too. 'You were such a help, Rupert! You probably have no idea how many times dropping your name achieved miracles. Look after her.'

'I will. Why don't you let Tom look after you, Chas?'

Chas coloured delicately. 'We are—we are…' She hesitated.

'We're going to be together on Benindee in a few months' time,' Tom put in.

'Yippee!' Vanessa carolled. 'Just wait until I tell Mum.'

Three months later, Chas closed The Perfect Day wedding consultancy. It was the day after she'd got her last wedding to the altar.

She looked around her apartment. She was due to leave it the next day but most of her furniture, the stuff she loved, was going to Benindee.

She paused in what she was doing and watched the river from her bedroom window. She often felt like pinching herself these days. Who would have thought that Charity Bartlett would sell up, up sticks, to go and live with a man she still hadn't slept with, on an isolated Cape York property that grew cattle, coffee, peanuts and sugar cane?

It was like throwing everything into the wind, she reflected. She still hadn't completely resolved in her mind whether Tom had issued an ultimatum over her going to Benindee or sought a commitment from her to equal his.

'On the other hand,' she murmured, 'I have no doubt now that I'm in love with him. As for our future together? What will be will be.'

She looked back over the past three months. They'd met twice a month after he'd moved to Benindee but she'd spent quite a bit of time at Cresswell. Her family had met his family and her parents had been most impressed by Tom.

Of course, there were some reservations on both sides about the lack of a wedding but, as Chas had explained, more than once, it was such a change of lifestyle for her, they'd decided to wait. She'd told no one that they hadn't actually discussed marriage at all.

But her times together with Tom had been blissful. They'd lunched, dined, gone to concerts and the races, and they had reignited the things they did to each other but only up to a point, not a point of no return.

She was grateful for that although it grew increasingly hard for them both. On the other hand, it withdrew the pressure of her fears about how good she was in bed. In fact Tom's whole stance on the matter, so down-to-earth yet so capable of stirring her deeply, was an enormous help.

Without the strain of Vanessa's wedding hovering over them, it had all been a revelation and it was what she'd clung to in the in-between times, the times she'd felt like pinching herself.

The times—she had to be honest—when she couldn't help wondering if Tom was as deeply in love as she was.

Common sense told her that at least it wasn't marriage she was leaping into. Common sense told her that with her background it was the way to go, and not only hers but Tom's, on account of Sarah Oldfield…

She'd also prepared herself as well as she could for Benindee. She'd taken riding lessons from Harriet. Unbeknown to Tom, she'd also taken flying lessons. She'd formed the opinion that she might be a better flier than a rider but at least she'd started along the road of both.

She'd taken bread-making lessons from her father; she and her mother had shopped for boots, bush hats and clothes. She'd enrolled in a TAFE course in mechanics.

She'd wondered what she'd do with her spare time

at Benindee. Her mother had supplied a solution: photography. 'I think you'd have the right eye for composition, light factors and so on,' Hope had said.

Chas had drawn an excited breath. It was something she'd always wanted to do.

She came back to the present and turned away from her river view. She was having dinner with her parents tonight—her father had recovered and been persuaded to cut down on his workload. Tom was picking her up first thing in the morning.

Destiny awaits you, Chas Bartlett, she said to herself.

It wasn't Tom who picked her up, it was one of his pilots with the news that Tom had been delayed on Benindee due to a minor flood. They flew to Cairns in a Lear jet then transferred to a six-seater propeller craft for the last leg. It was a lovely flight over the coastline then swinging inland towards the Lakeland-Laura district and Benindee.

The size of the property was awesome. The country was beautiful, wild and scenic with a river threading through it glinting like steel beneath the sun, and a mountain, although they also flew over the newly planted coffee plantation—the peanuts and sugar cane hadn't gone in yet.

She'd asked the pilot, Paul, how even a minor flood might affect the airstrip. He'd told her that only the western half of the property had been affected, not the homestead and its environs. 'You get freakish rain like that up here,' he'd added.

Then he'd buzzed the homestead and Chas was surprised at its size. There was also a lawn around it and a swimming pool—she hadn't expected or been told about that.

Finally they touched down on the grassy strip and taxied towards a large shed housing another light plane and several vehicles. There was no one about.

Paul removed his headphones and frowned. 'Strange. Thought the boss would be sure to come and meet you.'

Chas felt a tremor of nerves. 'I hope nothing's happened to him.'

'I'll see if I can raise him on the VHF radio.'

In fact, before he got a chance to do that, there was an incoming message on his VHF radio.

The gist of the static-ridden conversation was that Tom and his party had been trapped by a rising creek about twenty miles from the homestead and wouldn't get back until the next morning at the earliest.

They were also in a poor radio reception and transmission area with a very limited range and that was why they hadn't been able to get the message out to anyone else. Therefore, since there was no one at the homestead, the pilot was to take Chas back to Cooktown, where she could stay in a motel, and come back the next day.

'Roger,' the pilot said into the mike. 'Alpha Kilo Quebec out.' He turned to Chas and grimaced. 'Sorry, but it can't be helped.'

Chas frowned. 'There's no reason I can't stay—one night on my own is not going to be a real hardship, surely!'

'Ma'am—Ms Bartlett, it's not worth my job to allow you to do that.'

'Paul, short of force, there's no way you can stop me, although I'd appreciate it if you'd help me to get up to the house. Believe me, I intend to do this and I will take full responsibility for it.'

Paul, who, like everyone else who worked for Tom Hocking, was wildly curious about the woman who was joining him on Benindee, looked into those deep blue eyes and got a bit of a shock. She meant every word of it!

Could it be that the boss had met his match? he wondered.

'There could be—' he gestured vaguely '—snakes and things.'

'Let's go and check it out,' Chas said. 'I'm not going back. You have no idea what I've achieved just to get here,' she added obscurely.

An hour or so later, she was on her own in the homestead, having driven the pilot back to the airstrip and waved him off.

They'd found no 'snakes and things'. They'd found plenty of food and water; Chas had demonstrated that she was capable of running the generator for power, and operating the gas stove. They'd established the presence of a satellite phone in case of emergencies, as well as a medical kit.

She looked around at her new domain. Further from Cresswell Lodge it could not be, but had an as yet slightly raw but definite charm of its own. It had a colonial feel to it, she decided, with deep, screened verandas all round, some lovely old steamer chairs, high ceilings with fans suspended from them and polished wooden floors throughout.

From the veranda, the mountain and the river Tom had told her about and she'd seen from the air were visible, surrounded by a vast, ancient plain. It was a beautiful view.

The house was indeed sparsely populated furniture-wise but the basics were there, and she recognised a couple of pieces from Cresswell. A mahogany hall table was one of them, and on it was a picture of her in the beige silk suit she'd worn for Vanessa's wedding—she hadn't even known it had been taken. It brought a smile to her lips and she blinked away a tear.

Although there wasn't a lot of furniture, there was every mod con you could wish for.

There were four bedrooms. The main one had a big bed and a mosquito net. It was slightly untidy—as if Tom had left in a rush. The bed wasn't made and some of his clothes were lying on the blue slate bathroom floor. The bathroom opened out onto a walled courtyard.

I could make that really picturesque, she thought, with pot plants and statues. I could make the whole house lovely.

She picked up his discarded clothes and closed her eyes as the essence of Tom Hocking assailed her senses. It's going to be all right, she thought. I feel at home.

As day passed into the swift closing of the tropics, she unpacked what she'd brought with her—most of it was still to arrive in a container with her furniture. She made a light meal for herself which she ate on the veranda.

It was so quiet and the stars were so bright, she was amazed. Then she yawned twice in quick succession and decided to take herself to bed.

Lights and the sound of a motor woke her.

She sat up, clutching the sheet, with a prickle of fear running through her. Then there were heavy footsteps on the veranda and they came into the house—she hadn't even tried to lock the doors, feeling sure it was a precaution one didn't need to take beyond the black stump.

It was the light of a torch that preceded the footsteps into the main bedroom and it cast a huge shadow on the wall.

Chas opened her mouth to scream—there was nothing else she could do. Then Tom said urgently, 'Chas? Are you all right?'

Before she could answer he flicked aside the mosquito net, dropped the torch onto the bedside table, sat down on the side of the bed and pulled her into his arms.

Tom!' She found her voice. 'You frightened the life out of me.'

'Same here.' His breath rasped in his throat and she realised his heart was beating almost as heavily as hers.

'But—but why?' she stammered. 'How did you know I was here?'

'Paul,' he said bitterly. 'He had no damn right to disobey my orders and leave you here alone.'

Chas sighed exasperatedly. 'I asked him not to let you know just in case you were worried.'

'Worried?' He looked into her eyes. 'Chas, I've had a lot of difficulty persuading myself you would actually come to Benindee, but to have to spend your first night here alone was the last thing I wanted for you.'

'So,' she whispered, her eyes huge, 'how…how did you get here?'

'Walked, swum, drove a vehicle we'd left on the other side of the creek through dangerous terrain, but I made it.'

Her lips parted as she studied him. His clothes were damp and filthy, the knuckles on one hand were grazed, there was a long scratch down his cheek.

'It meant so much to you? The fact that you didn't want me to be here on my own on my first night?'

'Yes. It meant the world. Listen, I'd planned to wait.' He closed his eyes briefly. 'I knew you needed time to get away from the past and adapt to the future but I can't wait any longer. I love you, I can't live without you. Will you marry me, Chas?'

The world stood still for Chas and it felt as if all the stars, so bright over Benindee, had fallen into her lap.

'Tom,' she breathed, 'do you mean that?'

He smiled with some irony. 'It's grown in me since the time you came into my bed by mistake. I tried to tell myself you were a prickly iron maiden—probably exactly what I didn't need in my life! I tried keeping out of your way and, just when I thought I was safe, the moment you walked back into my life I was back to square one, which was to say—' he grimaced '—ever more attracted.'

'When did you know it was love?'

'I had my suspicions from rather early on,' he said gravely. 'Uh—it started to crystallise when you dived into a pool in your sexy underwear in order to have the last word. Of course, I bumped into the hurdle of Benindee and your career almost immediately… Chas, can I tell you something?'

She nodded.

'I lost Sarah Oldfield because of this place but you struck a chord with me when you said that what was in the past seemed to have happened in another life, on a different planet. That's how I felt about Sarah, only my scars were completely healed, I discovered, whereas yours weren't.' He looked into her eyes steadily. 'Can I hope it's really happened for you now?'

'It's really happened for me, Tom,' she said huskily. 'Thank you so much for understanding and, yes, I would love to marry you.'

'Thank God,' he murmured and kissed her until it started to get out of hand.

'Uh…' He lifted his head and looked into her eyes with a naked glint of desire in his own as well as a tinge of rueful amusement. 'Maybe we should stop and—'

'No, maybe we shouldn't.' She cupped his face in her hands.

'And I should take a shower, I was going to say,' he said gravely.

She shook her head. 'It's not that kind of night. It's an all or nothing, now or never night tonight—but you can take your clothes off.'

'Yes, ma'am. Don't tell me…' His gaze fastened on her nightgown, a slip of cranberry silk he recognised only too well. 'You're wearing our nightgown!'

Chas had to laugh. 'I often wear it, especially when I'm lonely and a long way from you. It's almost like being in your arms. I don't know what I'll do when it wears out.'

He took an unsteady breath. 'You'll have me,' he pointed out. 'May I?'

She nodded and put her arms up so he could draw the cranberry silk over her head.

'Oh, Chas,' he said, and drew his hands down her body, 'if you only knew.'

'What?' she asked huskily.

His lips twisted. 'How much I want you.'

'Same here.' She sighed suddenly. 'I thought three months was never going to end.' She buried her head in his shoulder. 'Love me, please, Tom.'

* * *

It was a clear, beautiful dawn that broke over Benindee.

They watched it through the bedroom window in each other's arms, in bed.

'The first day of the rest of our lives,' Tom said.

'Mmm… Thank you, again.'

He raised an eyebrow and smoothed her hair. 'What for?'

'Proving that some romantic myths are not myths at all.'

She felt his chest jolt with silent laughter.

'No, I'm serious.'

'Chas, that was us, not just me. Although, for the record, I am dedicated to your welfare in that area. I always will be.'

'That's lovely. The same could be said for me, of course.' She stroked her hand down his chest.

He took an unexpected breath then nudged her gently over onto her back and gathered her wrists in one hand to position them above her head. 'ICC, or not so instantaneous?' he queried with pure devilry in his grey eyes.

'I have a choice?'

'Not if you keep doing that.'

What she'd done was stretch luxuriously right down to her toes and wriggle her body sensuously on the sheet.

'I'll stop, then,' she murmured seriously. 'How about an ECC?'

He narrowed his eyes. 'Extra, or…eventual CC?'

She nodded.

'It's too late for that,' he informed her. He was right. They came together swiftly, joyfully, and if the ground didn't rock, it certainly felt like it.

'Of course,' he said afterwards, when they were catching their breath, 'we have the rest of our lives for all manner of CCs. Slow and dreamy as well. Tell me something.' He smoothed her hair and gathered her close. 'For an ex-wedding consultant extraordinaire, how do you see our wedding?'

She thought for a moment, then told him.

He blinked. 'Sure?'

'Never been more sure. How about you?'

He cupped her face and kissed her lips. 'I'm actually enchanted by the idea. It has a certain cachet, a certain uniqueness that's pure Chas Bartlett. It also means I won't have to wait too long.'

She laughed up into his eyes. 'Or me!'

All the same, it took two weeks to organise but it was a wonderful time for Chas. She got to know her new home, she got to demonstrate some of her new skills to Tom.

'Holy mackerel!' he said. 'Although I don't know why I should be surprised. You never do anything by halves.'

They were on the veranda watching the sun set while having a pre-dinner drink. Chas had just confided the fact that she'd taken some flying lessons to him.

'I was a bit worried about the flying,' she said ruefully, 'not exactly being renowned for my sense of direction, but, with all the instruments, it's actually a lot easier than I thought.'

He reached for her hand. 'Do you have any idea how grateful I am for your poor sense of direction?'

Chas controlled a desire to smile. 'Do you have any idea how you embarrassed the life out of me, not only then, but later?'

He rubbed his jaw. 'You never failed to blush, Aphrodite.'

Right on cue a faint tide of colour rose into her cheeks.

He tightened his grip on her hand. 'I can still do it?'

'Still,' she agreed. 'Maybe you always will.'

'I love that.'

'What this place needs,' Chas said one morning when they were driving out to a bore, 'is Leroy.'

Tom grimaced and swung the wheel to avoid a boulder. 'I didn't think he was your favourite dog.'

'On the contrary, I have very fond memories of Leroy.'

'So do I.' He put his arm around her shoulder. 'Still, we wouldn't want to put Adam out of a job, and Piccanin would pine.'

'Just a thought,' Chas said.

Then it was the eve of their wedding day and Chas looked around her in some amazement. She felt as if she'd been on Benindee for a lot longer than two weeks.

She'd embraced the lifestyle, she'd got to know everyone employed on the property; she was never bored for a moment. She'd started to take over some of the paperwork; she'd advertised for a married couple to help her with the homestead and the garden; she'd begun her new hobby of photography.

If there was one thing she was going to have to come to grips with, it was the heat. Winter, as it was now, was lovely but if this was winter and required the lightest of clothes, what was midsummer going to be like?

But the country itself was drawing her in too. The

colours, the feeling of space and freedom, the history. And the arrival of her furniture, plus some more she'd ordered, saw the house taking shape nicely.

Most of all, even only a fortnight of living with Tom had been deeply satisfying. Their ardour was still white-hot.

'How we stayed out of each other's beds for as long as we did never ceases to amaze me,' he said with a lurking grin that evening.

They were having dinner by candlelight and sharing a bottle of wine. Chas had concocted a delicious risotto.

'I've never told you this…' she paused and looked wry '…but I had the greatest difficulty convincing myself that I hadn't been, well, meant for your bed all along. After I hopped into it by mistake.'

'I've never told *you* this,' he echoed, 'but after you hopped into my bed by mistake, I was never quite the same man again. I used to get these visions of you at the most inconvenient moments. It was a great trial to me.'

'Oh. Good!' She laughed at his expression. 'I mean, at least I wasn't alone in—' she gestured '—you know.'

'Amazing fantasies?' he suggested.

'Yes. Even whipped cream, and other delights,' she said somewhat darkly, and told him about her father's Herb Alpert record.

'Well, well,' he drawled. 'I—'

'Don't you dare make anything of it, Tom Hocking!' she warned.

'OK, no whipped cream but I may surprise you in other ways.' He continued to eat his dinner serenely.

Chas took a sip of wine. 'How?'

'You'll just have to wait and see.'

She rested her elbow on the table and her chin on her hand. She'd changed into a light long dress and tied her hair back.

'Tom,' she said slowly, 'am I right in thinking you feel like a new man?'

His eyebrows rose. 'If I haven't demonstrated that to you by now, Aphrodite—'

'No,' she interrupted quietly. 'I mean, yes, you have, in that regard. I meant otherwise. This has been a huge change of lifestyle for you as well. Are you happy with it?'

He sat back and raised his glass to his lips. 'Chas...yes, I do feel like a new man. I was getting fairly frustrated with Cresswell. Of course, it means a lot to me, but actually it means more to Vanessa and my mother. Not that I'll ever let it go. We may even find that we spend some time there each year to escape the worst of the heat up here.'

'Good idea. Would it have had something to do with making your own mark, your own territory? Your sense of frustration?'

'Probably,' he agreed. 'I think I'll always see Cresswell as my father's creation—my grandfather and great-grandfather's too, come to that—but I needed to strike out on my own. Actually, Benindee came into the family via my great-grandmother. Her father was an explorer all over the Cape York-Gulf country. I think some of his genes must have come down to me.'

'I'm glad you did. I'm glad I'm with you.'

His eyes rested on her and softened. 'You couldn't be happier about it than I am.'

She slept on her own that night. He made no demur although he held her extra tightly before they parted.

Her last thought before she fell asleep was that she had no idea what she would be wearing to her wedding tomorrow.

They arrived early. They'd only flown from Cooktown, where they'd spent the night in a motel.

'They' were her mother and father, Harriet and Clare Hocking, Lord and Lady Weaver. They brought with them a mountain of stuff, including one mysterious package that was whisked out of sight.

It was an ecstatic reunion even though Chas had only been gone for a fortnight. Then the women of the party shooed Tom, her father and Rupert out of the house and told them to take a tour of the property.

It had only taken Chas one simple phone call to achieve it. 'Mum,' she'd said down the line to Hope Bartlett, 'can you organise my wedding for me? I'm sure Harriet, Clare and Vanessa will help.'

They'd brought the food, they'd brought decorations, they'd brought the wedding outfit.

'Oh, Mum,' Chas said with tears in her eyes as she gazed at it, 'it's perfect.'

'Darling,' Hope hugged her, 'I knew you wanted something different, and I knew you wanted something appropriate for up here—I could just see you in this.'

The two-piece outfit consisted of a caftan top with three-quarter sleeves, about hip-length, in a gauzy wild-mushroom pink, and was embroidered heavily around the wide cuffs and neckline with small pewter beads. The trousers were satin, the same colour, and flaring below the knees. The pewter sandals that came with the outfit were high and strappy. It was the last word in elegance and perfect for an outback bride.

'I see where you get your great taste from, Chas,' Vanessa enthused. 'OK, let's get started, troops!'

Several bubbly hours later, just as the flying-doctor plane delivered the pastor who was to perform the service to the airstrip, the bride and her party were ready.

Clare and Harriet wore their outfits from Vanessa's wedding, Vanessa wore her going-away outfit. As usual, Hope Bartlett looked superb, in oyster silk. The men had been readmitted to the house but the bride and the bridegroom had been kept apart.

The table on the veranda bore champagne, a wedding cake and a feast of finger food. There were white ribbon streamers and posies of dried flowers. There was a smaller table with an exquisite embossed taffeta cloth for the marriage service. There was even Handel's *Water Music* playing softly in the background.

Chas and her father stood in a bedroom, awaiting their cue.

'Nervous, sweetheart?' her father asked. 'You look wonderful!'

Chas looked down at her beautiful outfit. It might have been made for her. 'No, Dad.'

'Why the suspicion of tears, then?' he asked gently.

'Because I love you and I love Mum and how you've done all this for me. And because sometimes I thought I would never love a man again.'

'But you do?'

'Very, very much.'

He hugged her. 'We're so happy for you, Chassie. Oh, here we go!'

It was Loretta Quinn's beautiful harp music that accompanied Chas and her father. All she carried was the perfectly pressed cream rosebud from Vanessa's bouquet, mounted on a heart-shaped, beaded backing.

Tom, with Rupert by his side, turned as she came onto the veranda on her father's arm. Tom had also dispensed with tradition. He wore fawn trousers, a long-sleeved dark brown linen shirt and a coppery tie. He stood quite still as he watched her come to him, with stunned admiration in his eyes.

Then the service began and before long they were pronounced man and wife. Chas now wore a beautiful sapphire engagement ring and a plain gold wedding band.

'You may kiss the bride,' the pastor said with a wide smile.

'Does he know just how afflicted I am with a desire to kiss the bride?' Tom queried with some alarm against the side of her mouth.

'I…'

'I knew you'd be different. I didn't know you'd be so perfectly, gorgeously different.'

'Tom,' she breathed, 'thank you but everyone's waiting.' Then she paused and frowned. 'Was that a dog I heard?'

'Ah. I think I will kiss you first.' He did, and the congregation cheered.

They broke apart laughing and then they were surrounded by their excited, loving families.

For all that it was small, it was quite a wedding party. Vanessa and Rupert were obviously very happy, and imparted the news that a baby was on the way.

Harriet took Chas aside and told her she couldn't have found a more perfect partner for Tom if she'd gone out and hand-picked one.

'I have to say,' Chas replied, 'that even before I was

a hundred per cent sure about my feelings for Tom, I thought you'd make a wonderful mother-in-law!'

Clare presented them with a huge antique porcelain dinner service.

So lively was the party, in fact, Chas forgot about the dog she thought she'd heard until Tom cleared his throat and said, 'I haven't given Chas her present yet. Rupert, would you mind doing the honours?'

Harriet rolled her eyes. 'If you only knew what we went through with your present, Chas!'

'Indeed,' Clare said. 'Diamonds or pearls would have been much easier to handle!'

'Oh,' Vanessa waved a hand, 'I'm sure they'll come.'

Rupert reappeared at that point, staggering slightly under the weight of a closed wicker basket. He put it down at Chas's feet and, a bit like a magician, opened the lid with a flourish.

Chas stared downwards, transfixed. There was a miniature Leroy in it. Which was to say, since it was a Great Dane puppy about eight weeks old, miniature was only a relative term.

'Oh, my!' She gazed down at the puppy, who sat up and experimented with another bark.

'He's actually a brother of Leroy's, two litters later.'

'Oh, sweetheart!' Chas knelt down beside the basket. 'Aren't you handsome?'

'Maybe this wasn't such a good idea,' Tom murmured, and everyone laughed.

'I've just thought of the perfect name for him.' Chas looked up radiantly. 'Luke Longley. You know how Leroy is named after Leroy Loggins?'

'Another lanky basketball player. Perfect,' her father contributed and raised his glass. 'To Luke!'

They all drank a toast to the puppy, then scattered as he leapt out of his basket, collided with a lamp table, knocked it over and retreated yelping under the main table.

'This could be the story of our lives for a couple of months,' Tom complained.

'Maybe, but thank you so much!' Chas stood on her toes and kissed him.

As the sun set on their wedding day, Tom and Chas sat on the top veranda step. They were alone. Their families had flown back to Cairns for the night, then would go on south in the morning.

'Happy, Mrs Hocking?' Tom asked.

They still wore their wedding clothes. She put her hand on his knee and studied her new rings. 'Terribly happy. How about you?'

'Do you remember saying to me once that what I lacked in my life was some kind of rock—maybe a wife and children?'

'Yes, I remember.'

'I always thought this was going to be the rock.' He gestured over the landscape layered with pink and blue tinges as the sun slipped away. Then he put his arm round her and his voice was uneven as he continued. 'I was wrong. It's you, Chas.'

She laid her head on his shoulder with her heart beating heavily with love and wonder, with the knowledge that there were no barriers left between them. 'It's us, Tom.'

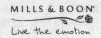

FREE!
4 Books
and a surprise gift!

We would like to take this opportunity to thank you for reading this Mills & Boon® book by offering you the chance to take FOUR more specially selected titles from the Modern Romance™ series absolutely FREE! We're also making this offer to introduce you to the benefits of the Reader Service™—

- ★ **FREE home delivery**
- ★ **FREE gifts and competitions**
- ★ **FREE monthly Newsletter**
- ★ **Exclusive Reader Service offers**
- ★ **Books available before they're in the shops**

Accepting these FREE books and gift places you under no obligation to buy, you may cancel at any time, even after receiving your free shipment. Simply complete your details below and return the entire page to the address below. You don't even need a stamp!

YES! Please send me 4 free Modern Romance books and a surprise gift. I understand that unless you hear from me, I will receive 6 superb new titles every month for just £2.80 each, postage and packing free. I am under no obligation to purchase any books and may cancel my subscription at any time. The free books and gift will be mine to keep in any case.

P6ZEF

Ms/Mrs/Miss/Mr ....Initials...................

Surname .... **BLOCK CAPITALS PLEASE**

Address..

....

....Postcode ....

Send this whole page to:
UK: FREEPOST CN81, Croydon, CR9 3WZ